KU-132-984

CONTENTS

PRAISE FOR
DICK KING-SMITH

'Sparkling humour and wonderful
characters are Dick King-Smith's trademarks'
Books for Your Children

'Dick King-Smith has brought magic into
the lives of millions of children'
Parents Magazine

'Here is an author who has earned his stripes
in the world of animal writing so you
know you'll be in for a good read'
Belfast Telegraph

'The king of animal stories, King-Smith uses his
language skills to the full to engage readers'
Birmingham Post

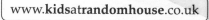

www.**kidsatrandomhouse**.co.uk

**Also available by Dick King-Smith,
award-winning author of *Babe*:**

From Corgi Pups, for beginner readers
Happy Mouseday

From Young Corgi
The Adventurous Snail
Billy the Bird
Connie and Rollo
E.S.P.
Funny Frank
Omnibombulator
Titus Rules OK

From Corgi Yearling Books
A Mouse Called Wolf
Mr Ape
Harriet's Hare

From Corgi Books, for older readers
Godhanger
The Crowstarver

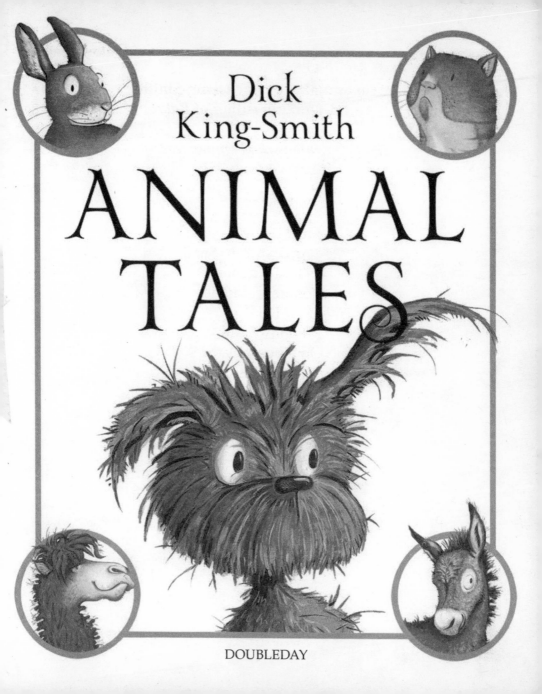

Dick
King-Smith

ANIMAL
TALES

DOUBLEDAY

ANIMAL TALES
A DOUBLEDAY BOOK
HARDBACK: 978 0 857 53093 6
TRADE PAPERBACK: 978 0 857 53128 5

ALL BECAUSE OF JACKSON
First published in Great Britain by Doubleday, an imprint of Random House Children's Books.
Doubleday edition published 1995, Young Corgi edition published 1997, Young Corgi edition reissued 2006.
Text copyright © Foxbusters Ltd, 1995
Cover illustration copyright © Garry Parsons, 2006   Inside illustrations copyright © John Eastwood, 1995

THE CATLADY
First published in Great Britain by Doubleday, an imprint of Random House Children's books.
Doubleday edition published 2004, Young Corgi edition published 2005.
Text copyright © Foxbusters Ltd, 2004
Illustrations copyright © John Eastwood, 2004

THE GUARD DOG
First published in Great Britain by Doubleday, an imprint of Random House Children's Books.
Doubleday edition published 1991, Young Corgi edition published 1992, Young Corgi edition reissued 2006.
Text copyright © Foxbusters Ltd, 1991
Cover illustration copyright © Garry Parsons, 2006   Inside illustrations copyright © Jocelyn Wild, 1988

HAIRY HEZEKIAH
First published in Great Britain by Doubleday, an imprint of Random House Children's Books.
Doubleday edition published 2005, Young Corgi edition published 2006.
Text copyright © Foxbusters Ltd, 2005
Cover illustration copyright © Garry Parsons, 2005   Inside illustrations copyright © John Eastwood, 2005

HORSE PIE
First published in Great Britain by Doubleday, an imprint of Random House Children's Books.
Doubleday edition published 1993, Young Corgi edition published 1994, Young Corgi edition reissued 2006.
Text copyright © Foxbusters Ltd, 1993
Cover illustration copyright © Garry Parsons, 2006   Inside illustrations copyright © Valerie Littlewood, 1993

This collection first published in Great Britain as ANIMAL TALES by Doubleday,
an imprint of Random House Children's Books. A Random House Group Company

This edition published 2011

1 3 5 7 9 10 8 6 4 2

Copyright © Foxbusters Ltd, 2011

The right of Dick King-Smith to be identified as the author of this work has been
asserted in accordance with the Copyright, Designs and Patents Act 1988.

All rights reserved. No part of this publication may be reproduced, stored in a retrieval system,
or transmitted in any form or by any means, electronic, mechanical, photocopying, recording or otherwise,
without the prior permission of the publishers.

The Random House Group Limited supports the Forest Stewardship Council (FSC®), the leading international forest-certification organisation.
Our books carrying the FSC label are printed on FSC®-certified paper. FSC is the only forest-certification scheme endorsed by the leading
environmental organisations, including Greenpeace. Our paper-procurement policy can be found at www.randomhouse.co.uk/environment.

MIX
Paper from
responsible sources
FSC® C016897
www.fsc.org

RANDOM HOUSE CHILDREN'S BOOKS
61–63 Uxbridge Road, London W5 5SA

www.kidsatrandomhouse.co.uk
www.randomhouse.co.uk

Addresses for companies within The Random House Group Limited can be found at:
www.randomhouse.co.uk/offices.htm

THE RANDOM HOUSE GROUP Limited Reg. No. 954009

A CIP catalogue record for this book is available from the British Library.

Printed and bound by CPI Group (UK) Ltd, Croydon, CR0 4YY

Dick King-Smith

All Because
of Jackson

Illustrated by John Eastwood

TOWER HAMLETS LIBRARIES	
91000000970913	
Bertrams	28/10/2011
JF	£9.99
THISWM	TH11001582

CHAPTER ONE

Jackson was a seaside rabbit.

He was born in a sandy burrow on top of a cliff, and as soon as he was old enough to come out and sit on the grass and look down at the sea, he was fascinated by it.

While his brothers and sisters played about in the clifftop field, Jackson would sit by himself and watch the waves rolling in to break upon the sandy shore.

He watched the tides go in and out, he watched the seabirds wheeling and diving, and especially he watched the tall sailing-ships gliding past in the distance. How beautiful they are, thought Jackson. How I should love to run away to sea and be a sailor.

He consulted his mother.

"Mama," he said.

"Yes, Jackson?"

"There are men on those ships, aren't there?"

"Yes, Jackson. Sailors."

"I should like to be a sailor, Mama."

"Silly boy," said Jackson's mother. "Rabbits don't go on ships."

"But, Mama, the sea is in my blood."

"You go on a ship," said his mother, "and your blood will be in the sea. Men eat rabbits."

Jackson went away to think about this. I could hide, he thought. There must be lots of places to hide in a big sailing-ship. I could be a stowaway. I won't tell Mama or Papa. I'll just go.

So he did.

Dick King-Smith

He set off across the clifftop field very early one morning, determined to find where the sailing-ships came in. That evening, climbing wearily to the top of a far headland, he looked down and saw before him just what he wanted.

There below was a wide bay, and on its shores a large seaside town with a great

harbour, in which lay a number of tall ships.

Tired out, Jackson found an empty rabbit burrow and crawled into it.

"Tomorrow," he murmured as he drifted into sleep, "tomorrow I shall go aboard my ship."

CHAPTER TWO

That night Jackson had the weirdest dream.

He was, it seemed, in a strange country, not cool and rainy like his homeland, but dry and very hot. Suddenly he saw the most extraordinary animal.

It was as tall as a man, with reddish fur, ears like a donkey, and a face like a sheep. Its arms were short, and it stood upright, balanced upon two enormously strong legs and a long, thick tail. Then the dream turned into a nightmare, for the monstrous creature began to come towards him, not walking, nor running, but hopping in huge bounds on those great hind legs. And as it drew near, Jackson could see something even more frightening. On the animal's stomach was a sort of pocket, and out of this pocket poked another head, with ears like a baby donkey and a face like a lamb!

Jackson woke with a squeal of terror.

"What's eating you?" said a voice, and there beside him in the burrow was

another rabbit, a young doe of about his own age.

"I was having a bad dream," he said.

"In my burrow," said the other.

"Oh, sorry!" said Jackson. "I didn't know. By the way, my name's Jackson."
"Funny sort of name."

"Not really. My father's called Jack. Anyway, who are you?"

"My mother doesn't believe in naming

children," said the young doe. "She's had so many, she can't be bothered. She just calls us all 'Bunny'."

"Bunny?" said Jackson. "That's nice. I like it." And I like you, he thought. I wonder if . . .

"You don't fancy going to sea, do you, Bunny?" he said.

"To sea?"

"In a ship. To sail away over the ocean."

"Where to?" said Bunny.

"I don't know," replied Jackson. "That'll be half the fun of it, not knowing."

"But rabbits don't go on ships," said Bunny.

"This one's going to," said Jackson.

"I want to sail the seas. I want to see the world."

"You're crazy," Bunny said. But nice, she thought.

"Well," she said, "it'll be daylight before very long. We'd better get started."

When they reached the town, Jackson and Bunny hopped through the empty silent streets until, as dawn was breaking, they reached the docks.

"Look!" cried Jackson as they made
their way along the cobbled quay.
"There's a ship!"

Tied up alongside was a great three-
masted sailing-ship, whose sides
towered above the two little rabbits.

"How ever shall we get aboard?" said
Bunny.

"The same way that the sailors do," said Jackson. "Follow me!" And he ran along the quay until he reached the foot of a long, narrow, wooden gangplank. It was nearly broad daylight by now and there were noises on board, bangings and knockings and men's voices and footsteps.

"Quick!" said Jackson. "Up we go!"
And up they went, scampering up the
gangplank on whose side was fixed a
large printed notice.

Brave British Hearts!
To all those of an
Adventurous Spirit
wishing to seek their fortunes
and start a new life in a
far country, take note that the
Peninsular & Oriental
Navigation Company's Clipper
Atalanta
will set sail for
AUSTRALIA
on the
Third day of April 1842

The moment that Jackson and Bunny reached the top of the gangplank, they saw to their horror a number of sailors busy swabbing down the decks. Luckily the men's backs were towards the two rabbits, who instantly dashed for cover.

A frightened rabbit goes straight underground, and though here there was no ground to go under, Jackson saw nearby a large, square, black hole, and into it he dived head first, Bunny following. Down the hatch they fell.

As well as passengers, the *Atalanta* was carrying in her hold goods for the settlers in Australia, and, luckily for the rabbits (for they fell a long way), it was a

cargo of bales of cloth. On these Jackson and Bunny landed and bounced.

"Are you all right, Bunny?" gasped Jackson.

"Yes, I think so. Where are we?"

"In a very big burrow by the look of things," said Jackson. "A good place for us to stow away, I should think."

"Would you?" said Bunny.

"Well, yes. We can hide amongst all this

stuff. No-one will ever find us. We can spend the whole voyage down here."

"And at the end of the voyage," said Bunny, "how exactly do we get out again?"

Jackson looked up at the open hatch, high above. He scratched one ear thoughtfully with a hind foot.

"Ah," he said.

"And while we're down here," went on Bunny, "what exactly do we eat?"

"Ah," said Jackson again.

"Or drink?"

"Ah," said Jackson. "Yes. Hm." But before he could add to this, they heard the sound of footsteps on the deck above, and voices, and then suddenly the square of daylight vanished as the hatch cover was put back, leaving the hold of the ship in darkness.

"It had better be a very short voyage," said Bunny. "Otherwise it would seem to me that, without food or water, we shall not see much of the world after all. We shall simply die down here. And all because of you, Jackson."

CHAPTER FOUR

All that morning the two rabbits hopped about in the gloom, exploring the great stack of bales of cloth that covered the floor of the hold, and finding nothing else.

Above them, there was much hustle and bustle on deck as the passengers came aboard, and then, around midday, a sudden great crash of sound as a brass band struck up on the quayside.

In amongst its noise the rabbits could hear voices bellowing orders, and the cries of farewell of those who were leaving and of those who had come to wave them goodbye.

Then, when the music had stopped and the shouts and calls had died away, peace and quiet returned as the *Atalanta* nosed her way out of harbour, and set sail for her journey to the opposite side of the world.

Down in the hold, Jackson and Bunny felt the motion as the clipper met the open sea, and heard the creaking of her timbers. Squatting side by side on a bale of cloth, the rabbits rose and fell as the ship swooped and dipped over the waves.

"Jackson," said Bunny.

"Yes?"

"I don't feel very well."

"Me neither."

"I don't think I'm a very good sailor."

"Nor me."

"I wish I hadn't come."

"Me too," said Jackson. "I'm sorry I got you into all this, Bunny. It's all my fault. I shall regret it for the rest of my life."

Bunny snuggled up to him.

"Don't worry," she said. "That won't be long."

By the following day the rabbits had grown used to the motion of the ship. They had also grown extremely hungry and thirsty.

When the ship had been some days at sea, the captain ordered an inspection of the various holds, to see that each was watertight and that their cargo had not shifted.

By now too weak and miserable to care, the rabbits watched helplessly as the hatch cover was removed, and a seaman climbed down a ladder, carrying a lantern.

A big, bearded man, he shone the light about as he examined the bales of cloth, and then its beam fell full upon the wretched stowaways.

"Well, I never!" said the seaman softly. "You'll make a nice meal, my hearties, you will!"

CHAPTER FIVE

Afterwards, Jackson and Bunny couldn't really remember what happened, so weak and helpless were they.

In fact, the bearded seaman found a sack and popped them in it, and climbed the ladder out of the hold, only to meet the first mate at the hatchway.

"All shipshape down below, Jenkins?" said the mate.

"Aye, aye, sir," replied Jenkins.

"What have you got in that sack?"

The seaman heaved a sigh.

He'll have 'em off me, he thought, that's for sure.

"Rabbits, sir," he said.

"Rabbits?" said the mate.

"Yes, sir," said Jenkins. "Found 'em in among the bales. Don't know how they come to be there."

The mate opened the mouth of the sack and peered in.

"Well, well!" he said. "They'll make a nice meal. Take them down to the galley

and tell the cook I'll have them for my supper."

"Aye, aye, sir," said Jenkins dolefully, but before he could move, the captain of the *Atalanta* appeared, an imposing figure with mutton-chop whiskers, a gold-peaked cap upon his head, and a brass telescope under his arm.

"What's all this, Mister Mate?" he said. "What has that man got in that sack?"

The first mate heaved a sigh. He'll have 'em off me, he thought, that's certain.

"Rabbits, sir," he said.

"Rabbits?" said the captain.

"Yes, sir," said the mate. "Open the sack, Jenkins."

"Well, well," said the captain. "I'm very partial to a nice young rabbit, or better still, two nice young rabbits, under a good, light, pastry crust, with some strips of fat bacon."

He put a hand into the sack and felt the limp forms within.

"Found 'em down below, did you, Jenkins?" he said.

"Yes, sir."

"Heaven only knows how they got there," said the captain, "but one thing's sure. They'll have had no food or water since we sailed. They're as weak as kittens. We must put some flesh on them first. Jenkins, take them to my cabin steward and tell him to see to their needs."

"Aye, aye, sir," said the seaman.

"And Mister Mate," said the captain, "I'd be obliged if you'd have a word with the ship's carpenter. Tell him to knock me up a cage for my rabbits, and to bring it up to my cabin when it's done."

"Aye, aye, sir," said the mate.

"One thing's sure," said the captain. "Once my rabbits have grown a bit and fattened up, they'll be well worth waiting for. I shall enjoy them, Mister Mate. They'll make a nice meal."

CHAPTER SIX

By great good fortune, the captain's cabin steward was a rabbit fancier. Ashore, he kept a shed full of tame ones, and under his expert care Jackson and Bunny soon recovered their health and strength.

Amongst the stores of food that the *Atalanta* had loaded for her voyage was a plentiful supply of vegetables, still fresh, and the two young rabbits gorged happily on cabbage-leaves and carrot-tops and turnip-greens.

In addition, the steward fed them

broken bits of ship's biscuit, and generally looked after them very well. In due
course, he knew, the captain would eat
them, but that was what rabbits were for.

"Tuck in, my dears," he said, stroking
their brown backs. "Enjoy life while you
can."

And indeed they did.

"It's funny, you know," said Jackson to
Bunny. "Mama told me that men eat
rabbits, but that doesn't seem to be true."

"They're certainly treating us well,"

said Bunny with her mouth full. "Both the little one who feeds us and the big one with the whiskers who stands and stares at us. I'm really quite enjoying this voyage now."

"Me too," said Jackson. "I wonder where we shall end up?"

In the captain's pie-dish was of course the answer to this question, and some weeks later the cabin steward's expert advice was sought.

"You keep rabbits at home, Tompkins, don't ye?" said the captain.

"Yes, sir."

"What d'ye think of these two now? Fit to eat, would you say?"

"Well, sir," said the steward, "they're not yet fully grown. I don't reckon they were more than two month old when they come aboard. And we've been at sea eight weeks – that makes 'em four months old now."

"Another four weeks' sailing," said the captain, "and we'll reach Australia. I want to make a meal of them before then."

"Was you going to eat the both of them yourself, sir?" asked the steward.

I was, thought the captain, when they were littler, but now . . . maybe I should give a little dinner, for Sir Hereward and his lady, with rabbit-pie as the main course.

Sir Hereward Potts was a rich and important merchant in the city of London, sailing to Australia with the

intention of becoming the richest and most important merchant in the city of Sydney. He was much the most notable of the *Atalanta*'s passengers. A favourable report to the Peninsular and Oriental Navigation Company from Sir Hereward Potts would do the captain no harm at all, and the rabbit-pie would do Sir Hereward a power of good.

"Eat both of them myself, Tompkins?" said the captain in reply to the steward's question. "Of course not. I shall invite Sir Hereward and Lady Potts to share such a treat."

That evening the captain of the *Atalanta* asked the merchant and his wife to his cabin for a glass of wine, and proposed the little dinner party.

"Tomorrow, at about this hour?" he said. That should give Tompkins ample time to see to the preparation of the pie, he thought.

"Delighted, Captain," said Sir Hereward.

"Too kind," said Lady Potts.

Then she caught sight of Jackson and Bunny, lolloping happily about in their cage.

"Oh!" she cried. "How I do love rabbits!"

"So do I," said the captain.

"They are to be the main attraction of our little dinner tomorrow. They are still young and should be very tender, I have no doubt."

Much to the captain's surprise, Lady Potts gave a little scream of horror.

"Oh, Captain!" she cried. "Oh, you could not! Surely you do not mean to kill those charming little creatures? Oh, I could not bear to think of such a thing, much less eat them. Oh, Hereward, must they be slain?"

"My wife is tender-hearted, Captain," said Sir Hereward, and he did not look best pleased.

The captain thought fast.

"I do apologize for suggesting such a thing, your Ladyship," he said. "I had not realized . . . so thoughtless of me."

Stupid woman, he thought, now I shan't be able to eat them, she'll be for ever asking me how they are. There's only one thing to do.

"Sir Hereward," he said with a little bow, "I wonder – would you permit me to present these animals to Lady Potts as a gift, in token of my esteem?"

Sir Hereward looked doubtful.

"The rabbit is unknown in Australia," went on the captain, "and the possession of these two specimens would be in keeping with your wife's position as a leader in colonial society."

Lady Potts gave another little scream, this time of delight, and cried, "Yes! Oh, Captain, yes, how kind of you. Pray have them removed to our quarters for the remainder of the voyage. We shall be delighted to have them, shall we not, Hereward?"

And though Sir Hereward Potts' word was law to thousands in the world of business, he knew better than to cross swords with his wife.

"Yes, my dear," he said. "Delighted."

Thus it was that for the remaining four weeks of the voyage of the *Atalanta* to the Antipodes, the stowaways found themselves in the lap of luxury. Jackson and Bunny were petted and fondled and fed upon the choicest of titbits, and allowed the freedom of the Potts' stateroom for much of the day, while, with dustpan and brush, a steward cleaned up behind them.

When at last, at the end of her three-month voyage, the clipper *Atalanta* entered Sydney Harbour, the rabbits were in beautiful condition: fat, sleek and strong.

Sir Hereward had taken a house in the country, some way outside Sydney, and to this he travelled by coach with his wife and all their many pieces of baggage. Among these was the rabbit cage, covered with a sheet to conceal the inmates from prying eyes, for Lady

Potts intended to surprise the colonials with her unusual pets.

When they arrived she insisted that the rabbit cage be unloaded first and placed upon the lawn.

"I must let my little friends stretch their legs," she said to her husband, and she removed the sheet and opened the door of the cage.

Jackson and Bunny hopped out and looked about them.

"We seem to have arrived," said Jackson.

"But where?" said Bunny.

"I have no idea."

"Will they not run away, my dear?" said Sir Hereward.

"Run away?" said Lady Potts. "What an idea! They are much too tame and

much too fond of me, are you not, my dears?" And she bent to stroke them.

"Bunny," said Jackson. "Are you thinking what I'm thinking?"

"Yes," said Bunny. "Let's go!" And side by side they raced away, the first rabbits ever to set foot upon Australian soil.

CHAPTER EIGHT

After all those months cooped up in the *Atalanta* it was sheer bliss to be out in the fresh air again, out in the sunshine (and very hot sunshine it was), and to be free once more.

Jackson and Bunny ran and ran, just for the joy of running, and leaped and twirled and buckjumped (or in Bunny's

case doejumped) in the highest spirits, delighted with one another.

When at last they stopped and looked about them, it was to see a countryside very different from their cool damp homeland. The grass was more brown than green, and the blue-gums looked nothing like English trees. The birds that they saw were strange too – screeching cockatoos and laughing kookaburras and flocks of parrakeets and budgerigars.

Then suddenly Jackson saw a large shape in the distance.

"Quick! Hide!" he said to Bunny, and they scurried for the shelter of some tussocky grass.

"What's the matter?" said Bunny. "You're trembling."

"My dream!" said Jackson. "Do you remember, when we first met in your burrow, I'd been having a bad dream?"

"Yes, I remember."

"Well," said Jackson, "here it comes!" And peering through the grass stems, Bunny saw the most extraordinary animal.

It was as tall as a man, with reddish fur, ears like a donkey, and a face like a sheep. Its arms were short, and it stood upright, balanced upon two enormously strong legs and a long thick tail. Then this monstrous creature began to come towards them, not walking, not running, but hopping in huge bounds on those great hind legs. And as it drew near, Bunny could see something even more

frightening. On the animal's stomach
was a sort of pocket, and out of this
pocket poked another
head, with ears like
a baby donkey
and a face like
a lamb!

"Don't move," whispered Jackson. "It may not see us." And the two rabbits froze, crouching low with ears laid flat back and eyes bulging with terror.

With one last hop the great red kangaroo landed right beside their hiding-place and looked down at them out of her mild sheep's eyes. From her pouch her joey looked down too.

"Ma," he said. "What kind of animals are those?"

"No idea, son," said the mother kangaroo. "Never seen such strange-looking creatures in my whole life. Hold tight now." And away she bounded.

"Fancy calling *us* strange!" said Bunny. "I never set eyes on such weird things as those before."

CHAPTER NINE

As time passed, Jackson and Bunny were to see a great many other odd-looking beasts. As well as kangaroos, they met wallabies and bandicoots and opossums and koalas and numbats and wombats and many more.

There were familiar creatures as well, like cattle and a great many sheep, but one sort of animal they never met.

"It's funny, isn't it?" said Jackson one day. "In this place where we've landed up, wherever it is, there are no other rabbits."

"No," said Bunny, "but there soon will be."

"I don't understand," said Jackson.

But a little later he did, for Bunny scratched herself a nest-burrow and there gave birth to five babies.

"Aren't they lovely!" said Jackson, and indeed, he must have liked babies, because by the end of the rabbits' first year in their new country, Bunny had produced four more litters, totalling twenty-two young in all, and by then she and Jackson were already great-grandparents!

After another year there were hundreds of rabbits in Australia, and then thousands, and then tens of thousands.

Jackson and Bunny lived happily (though not "ever after", because a rabbit's lifespan is not a long one), and by the time they died, peacefully, of old age, there were hundreds of rabbits. And before long

there were millions, and then countless millions, that colonized large stretches of the best land in Australia; a great multitude of rabbits that dug holes everywhere and damaged trees and crops, and ate all the grass meant for the sheep, and drove the Australian settlers to distraction. One of the great plagues in the history of the world it was. And all because of Jackson.

THE END

Dick King~Smith

The
Catlady

Illustrated by John Eastwood

CHAPTER ONE

On the morning of January 22nd 1901, Muriel Ponsonby had, living in her house, sixteen cats (including kittens). By the evening of that day another litter of kittens had been born, bringing the total to a round twenty.

This event was, as usual, recorded in a large book titled BIRTHDAY BOOK (CATS ONLY).

Miss Ponsonby, it should be explained, was an elderly lady living alone in a large country house that had belonged to her parents. Because she had always looked after them, she had never married, and after their deaths she had allowed her liking for cats full rein. To be sure, she gave away some of the many kittens that appeared, but nevertheless Ponsonby Place – for this was the name of the family home – was always swarming with cats.

Miss Ponsonby kept herself to herself and did not mix much with the local villagers, save to go now and then to the local shop to buy provisions for herself and the cats. Most felt she was harmless, a rather sweet old lady, but there were some who said she was a witch. Partly because of this she was known to one and all as "The Catlady".

In fact she was not a witch but simply a somewhat strange old woman with odd habits.

For example, she talked constantly throughout the day, to herself a listener might have thought. But this was no sign of madness. She was, of course, talking to her cats, and they talked back. Colonel Sir Percival Ponsonby and his wife had always addressed their daughter by a shortened version of her Christian name Muriel and all her cats used this. When spoken to, they would reply "Mu! Mu! Mu!".

Many would have found it odd to discover that she took all her meals with her cats. The long refectory table in the great dining-room was laid with a bowl for each adult cat and any kittens old enough to jump up on it, and the Catlady

would sit at the head with her own bowl before her. To be sure, she used a knife and fork and spoon, and afterwards wiped her lips with a napkin while the rest cleaned their faces with their paws. But on occasion, so as not to seem standoffish, she would fill a bowl with milk and lap from it.

At night-time she was kept very comfortable,

especially in the winter, for all those cats who wished – and many did – slept on her bed, providing her with a warm furry coverlet.

With her rather sharp features, green eyes, and grey hair tied back to show her somewhat pointed ears, Muriel Ponsonby looked much like a giant cat as she lay stretched beneath the purring throng.

Few people knew of her eating habits, for she had no servants, and only the doctor, called on a rare occasion when she was confined to bed, had ever seen the cat blanket. But no one at all knew the strangest thing about Miss Ponsonby, which was that she was a firm believer in reincarnation.

As a simple soldier, her father, who had served in the army in India, thought that the idea of reincarnation was a lot of nonsense, but he had talked about it to his daughter when she was a child. As she grew older Muriel came to believe, as Hindus do, that when a person dies, he or she is reborn in another body, and not necessarily a human one. She was sure that some of her feline companions had once been people she knew. Thus among her cats there was a Percival (her late father, she was certain, just the same whiskers), a Florence (her late mother), a Rupert and a Madeleine (cousins), a Walter and a Beatrice (uncle and aunt), as well as some newly departed friends. Ethel Simmons, Margaret Maitland and Edith Wilson (two tabbies and a black), all old schoolfriends of hers, had reappeared in feline form.

It was to these nine cats that Muriel Ponsonby chiefly spoke, and they replied by making typical cat noises like miaowing and purring. All were delighted to be living in comfort in Ponsonby Place, in the care of a human whom they had, in

their previous lives, known and loved.

Percival and Florence were of course particularly pleased at how well their only daughter had turned out.

"How fortunate we are, my dear," the Colonel said to his wife, "to be looked after by Muriel in our old age."

"Old age?" said Florence. "I think you tend to forget, Percival, that we have been reincarnated into new bodies and that ours are now comparatively young."

"You are right of course, Florence dear," Percival replied. "Why, we have our new lives ahead of us."

"And possibly other lives," said Florence.

"What do you mean?"

Florence rubbed her face against her husband's luxuriant whiskers. "We might have babies," she said.

Of course not all the kittens born in Ponsonby Place were reincarnations of human beings. Most were simply ordinary kittens born to ordinary cats, and were given names like Tibbles or Fluff. The Catlady could tell the difference merely by looking into their eyes once they were opened, and until this happened she did not attempt to name them.

So it was not for ten days that she examined the four kittens born on January 22nd 1901, the very day upon which Queen Victoria had died. Three of the kittens were tabbies, the fourth a ginger.

The Catlady picked up the tabbies first, looking to see what sex each was, and then peering into its newly-opened eyes.

"You're a tom," she said, three times, and, again three times, "Sorry, dear, you're only a cat."

But when she came to the fourth kitten, a small and dumpy one, expecting it to be another tom – for ginger kittens usually were – she found it to be a queen, as female cats are called. Then she

looked into its eyes, and caught her breath.

"Not just a queen," said the Catlady in a hoarse whisper, "but *the* Queen!"

Reverently she placed the ginger kitten back in its nest. "Oh, Your Majesty!" she said. "Reborn on the day you died! To think that you have come to grace my house!" and awkwardly, for she was not as young as she had been, she dropped a curtsy.

"Your humble servant, Ma'am," said the Catlady, and retired from the room, backwards.

CHAPTER TWO

Hastily the Catlady made her way from the room in the East Wing where this latest litter of kittens had been born, to the principal bedroom of Ponsonby Place. It was a spacious chamber where her parents had slept in their lifetime – their previous lifetime, that is – and which they, in their reborn shapes, still naturally occupied. Once the Colonel had been a fiery old soldier and his wife a bit of a battleaxe, and now no other cat ever dared cross this threshold.

The Catlady found them lying side by side in the middle of the great four-poster bed. Percival had been reincarnated as a white kitten that had grown into a very large and fat cat. His sweeping whiskers aped the military moustache of the human Percival. Florence was a tortoiseshell

with just the same small dark eyes that had once glinted behind Lady Ponsonby's pince-nez.

"Papa! Mama!" cried the Catlady excitedly (she could never bring herself to address them by their first names). At the sound of her voice they yawned and stretched themselves upon the fine silken bedspread with its pattern of damask roses, which was now much torn by sharp claws and dirtied by muddy feet.

"What do you think!" went on the Catlady. "Our dear departed Queen is come to stay! Edward VII may now be King of England but here at Ponsonby Place Victoria still reigns!"

"Mu," said Percival in a bored voice and Florence echoed "Mu", and they climbed off the four-poster and made their way down the curving staircase towards the dining-room, for it was time for tea.

How I wish Mama and Papa were still able to

speak the Queen's English – the King's English, I should say, mused the Catlady as, in the huge stone-flagged kitchen, she set about the task of filling a large number of bowls with a mixture of fish-heads and boiled rabbit and ox liver. For that matter, I wish that those others that have been reborn could speak too. How nice it would be to talk over old times with Uncle Walter and Aunt Beatrice, or chat about school-days with Ethel or one of the other girls.

Her thoughts were interrupted by a loud impatient miaowing from the waiting cats.

The Catlady sighed. "Coming, dears!" she called.

She sat at the head of the table, nibbling a biscuit. Later, when all had been cleared away and washed up, she would make herself a nice cup of tea, but at that moment she realized for the first time that she was not only lonely for human conversation but that she was tired.

The older I get, she thought, the more cats and so the more work I have, and it'll be worse soon. Both Cousin Madeleine and Edith Wilson are pregnant.

By the time she got to bed that night (after making her respects to the infant Queen Victoria) the Catlady had come to a decision. "There's only one thing for it, dears," she said to the patchwork quilt of different-coloured cats that covered her. "I shall have to get help."

Next day she composed an advertisement to be placed in the local newspaper, the *Dummerset Chronicle*. It was very short. It said:

For some days the Catlady waited, rather nervously, for replies. She had been a recluse for so many years now that she was not looking forward to the ordeal of interviewing a whole string of strange people.

She need not have worried. As soon as the locals of Dumpton Muddicorum read the Situations Vacant in the *Dummerset Chronicle* they said to each other, "Look at this then! It's the old Catlady, advertising for home help. What a job, eh? Great rambling place, crawling with cats, and stinking of them too no doubt, and as for her, well, if she ain't a witch she's as mad as a hatter! Anyone who applies for that needs their heads seeing to."

And no one did.

Muriel Ponsonby did not renew the advertisement. Perhaps it's just as well, she thought, I probably wouldn't have got on with the person.

I'll just have to manage somehow.

Nonetheless when shopping in the village, she did ask the shopkeepers if they knew of anyone suitable, but none of them did.

"Not at the moment, madam," said the butcher, tipping his straw hat to her, "but I'll be sure to let you know if I hear of anyone," and the others replied in the same vein. They winked at other customers when she had left their shops, and the customers smiled and shook their heads, watching her pedal rather shakily away on her tall black bicycle with the big wicker basket on the handle-bars.

Poor old dear, they thought. She needs some help, no doubt about that, but she'll be lucky to get anyone. Shame really, she's a nice old thing.

As for the village children, they sniggered behind their hands. "It's that old Catlady!" they whispered, and when she had gone by, they curled their fingers like claws and hissed and catcalled, pretending to scratch one another.

The weeks went by, and Cousin Madeleine and Edith Wilson both gave birth, one to four and one to six kittens. These were just ordinary kittens (for no one among the Catlady's family or friends had died), but with a total now of thirty animals in her house she found herself wishing very much that someone – anyone – had answered that advertisement.

By now the little tubby ginger female that was, its owner knew beyond doubt, the reincarnation of the late great Queen, was weaned. The Catlady found that, try as she would to treat all her animals alike, this one had already become special. She took to carrying her about, and had at long last decided what to call her.

After the first shock of finding who was within the little furry body, she had very gradually given up treating this kitten with such exaggerated respect. She stopped curtsying to it and backing out of the room. From first addressing it as "Your Majesty", she had then progressed to "Victoria", and later, so familiar did she now feel with this royal personage, to "Vicky".

The other cats, incidentally, on learning from the ginger kitten who she had been in her previous incarnation, treated her with much respect, Percival especially so, as in his former shape, his bravery in India had earned him the Victoria Cross.

One winter's day, when the snow lay deep around Ponsonby Place, there was a knocking on the great front door, and the Catlady went to see who it could be, Vicky perched upon her shoulder.

Muriel opened the door, expecting the postman, for no one else usually came all the way up the long drive to the house. But it wasn't the postman. Standing on the steps outside was a young girl, poorly clad and shivering with cold.

Though on the whole the Catlady preferred cats to people, she was of a kindly nature, and now she did not hesitate. "Come in! Come in!" she cried. "You'll catch your death, whoever you are. Come, follow me, I have a good fire in the drawing-room." As the girl followed her across the vast echoing hall, a host of cats watched curiously from doorway and stairway.

"Here, sit by the fire and warm yourself," said

the Catlady, "and I will go and make you a hot drink."

When she had done so and the girl had drunk and some colour had come back into her pinched face, the Catlady said, "Now, tell me, what can I do for you?"

As she said this, it occurred to her that perhaps the girl had come in answer to that old advertisement in the *Dummerset Chronicle*. I rather hope not, the Catlady said to herself. This is not the sort of person I had in mind. Not only is she badly dressed but her clothes are dirty, with bits of straw sticking to them.

The Catlady's face must have shown her distaste, for the girl stood up and said, "I won't trouble you any longer, madam. I'll be on my way now and thank you for your kindness."

She spoke with a Dummerset accent. A local girl, thought the Catlady. "Wait a moment," she said. "You knocked on my door so you must tell me what you wanted."

"I saw your lights," said the girl, "and what with the snow . . . and I was fair wore out . . .

and I hadn't eaten for quite a while . . . I just couldn't go any further."

"And you're not going any further now," said the Catlady decidedly. "Sit down again. I'll fetch you some food."

CHAPTER THREE

Muriel Ponsonby was not particularly interested in food. As long as her cats were well fed, she herself was content with very simple fare and seldom kept much in the house.

Now however she was not long in providing some good hot soup and some bread and cheese for the young stranger, and not until the girl had finished eating did she press her further.

"Now, tell me your name."

"If you please, madam," said the girl, "my name is Mary Nutt."

"But tell me, Mary," said the Catlady, "where are your parents?" Mary's not very old, she thought. Fourteen perhaps?

"Dead," Mary replied.

"Both?"

"Yes, madam. Mother died a month ago, and my father, he was killed in South Africa, fighting the Boers. He was a soldier, my dad was, a soldier of the Queen."

At this last word, Vicky jumped up onto the girl's lap, and Mary stroked her and added, "And the Queen's dead too now."

Yes and no, said the Catlady to herself.

To Mary she said, "I am very sorry for you. My father is . . . that is to say, was . . . a soldier."

And now he's a white cat, she thought.

"Thank you, madam," said Mary Nutt. "The fact is that since Mother died, I've had nowhere to live. These last weeks I've just been wandering about the countryside, sleeping in haystacks, as you can see, with no food to speak of, for I've no money. That was the first good meal I've had for many a day and I thank you for your kindness."

This telling of her troubles and the sight of Vicky snuggled down on the girl's lap would probably have been enough to make up the Catlady's mind anyway. But then something happened which absolutely decided her.

In through the drawing-room door marched the white cat Percival, straight up to the girl, and began to rub himself against her legs, purring like mad.

Mary Nutt put out a hand to stroke him. "Isn't

he handsome!" she said.

"You like cats, do you?" asked the Colonel's daughter.

"Oh yes!" replied the daughter of a trooper.

The Catlady looked at her, stroking with one

hand Colonel Sir Percival Ponsonby and with the other cuddling Victoria, Queen of the United Kingdom, Empress of India, and any doubts vanished. "I hope," she said, "that you will stay here with me, Mary, and help me to look after my family."

On that snowy day when Mary Nutt first set foot in Ponsonby Place, the house was as it had been for many years now. That is to say the floors were dirty, the ceilings cobwebby, the furniture dusty, the chair covers grubby, and the windows smeary.

The place was a paradise for cockroaches and woodlice and earwigs and beetles, and even, in the damper parts, for snails (though mice had the sense to keep well away).

On top of everything else the whole house stank of cat.

By springtime the change in Ponsonby Place was miraculous. The floors and the ceilings and the furniture were clean, the covers washed, the insects gone. If the Colonel and his Lady could have been reincarnated in human rather than feline form, the house would have looked to them just as it had been in their day. To be sure, there was still a smell of cat but, thanks to opening as many (clean) windows as possible when the weather allowed, it was much less strong now.

All this of course was due to the busy hands of Mary Nutt, who had turned out to be what the Catlady's mother would have called "a treasure".

At first from simple gratitude at being given a home and then because she quickly grew fond of the Catlady, Mary worked

from dawn to dusk in Ponsonby Place, dusting, scrubbing, washing and polishing, and indeed doing most of the cooking. Even more importantly from the Catlady's point of view, her new helper paid a lot of attention to all the cats, and, whenever she had a spare moment, it was spent grooming some happily-purring puss.

Percival and the rest spoke about her to each other with approval. "Good sort of girl, that, don't you think?" he said to Florence. "She's being a great help to Mu, what?" and his wife agreed, as did the uncle and aunt, the cousins and the schoolfriends. Only Vicky made no comment.

The Colonel cleared his throat.

"I hope you approve of the young servant, Your Majesty?" he said respectfully.

Vicky looked up at the big white cat with her usual haughty expression. "We have only one criticism," she replied.

"What is that, pray, ma'am?"

"We do not have enough attention paid to us. We are after all the most important cat in the house, in the land indeed. The girl should feed us first."

"Certainly she should, ma'am," said Percival, and once Vicky had left the room, he had a word with all the other cats.

From then on, to Mary's puzzlement and Muriel's delight, when the food bowls were put upon the long refectory table, no cat touched a mouthful of its food until the tubby ginger cat Vicky had finished her meal and jumped down.

Just as it should be, thought the Catlady. Her Majesty must eat first. Perhaps one of these days I'll tell Mary about reincarnation. The poor girl has lost both father and mother, or at least she thinks she has. It would surely be a comfort if I could persuade her that each of them is no doubt enjoying another life in another form.

Chapter Four

As time passed the relationship between the Catlady and her young orphaned helper strengthened.

Miss Muriel (as Mary now addressed her employer) became a kind of replacement for the girl's late mother despite the huge gap in age.

Equally, for the childless Catlady, this hardworking, affectionate, cat-loving girl was a great blessing. Especially because once again the cat population of Ponsonby Place was increasing. Margaret Maitland and Edith Wilson had, between them, another half dozen kittens so that now the total was thirty-six.

Miss Muriel was pleased with the new arrivals, Mary could see, though she did not understand why the Catlady had picked up each new kitten, peered into its eyes, and then said in a disappointed voice "Oh dear, you're just a cat."

Just another cat, Mary thought, and more work for me. She knew, because she'd been told, that when the Colonel and Lady Ponsonby had been alive, they had employed a cook, a parlourmaid, and three housemaids, and of course there had not been an army of cats in the place. If only I could persuade Miss Muriel, Mary thought, to get rid of some of them. Every bit of furniture is covered in cat hairs, in wet weather every floor is dotted with muddy little pawprints, there are

litter trays everywhere to be emptied and often the kittens don't use them. What can I do to get Miss Muriel to part with some of them?

As though in answer to this question, a cat walked into the room Mary was dusting. It was a tomcat, she could see from its big round face, and ebony in colour. A black male, thought Mary Nutt, and "Blackmail!" she said out loud.

Suppose I told Miss Muriel, she thought, that if a lot of the cats don't go, then I will? I wouldn't actually go, of course, I couldn't let her down like that when she's been so good to me, but it might just work. And we could shut up some of the rooms, so there'd be less cleaning to do. Let's just hope I can persuade her.

As things turned out, luck was to be on Mary's side. While she was plucking up the courage to tackle her employer, the Catlady was herself beginning to feel that perhaps there were rather too many cats in Ponsonby Place. It's not the

expense of feeding them, she said to herself, I don't mind that, and it's not the work involved, for now dear Mary prepares their food and washes their dishes and cleans out their litter trays. It's because of Vicky, I suppose, she's become so important to me (well, she would be, wouldn't she, she is . . . was . . . the Queen) that I don't pay as much attention to the others as I used to. Except for Papa and Mama, of course, and the relations and friends. But as for the rest of them, I suppose I could do without them. That cat blanket's getting too much of a thing. I'd sooner just have Her Majesty on the bed.

But then something happened that was to settle things for both Mary and Muriel. For some time the Catlady had been a trifle worried about her late mother (that is to say, about the tortoiseshell cat Florence within whose body Lady Ponsonby had been reincarnated) because she seemed to be getting a bit fat.

"Oh Mama," said the Catlady as she entered the master bedroom, carrying Vicky, "I shall have to feed you less. Just look at the tummy on you!"

Following her own advice, she looked more carefully and then gave a gasp of horror as the truth dawned upon her.

"Oh Mama!" she cried. "You are pregnant!"

Florence stretched languidly on the four-poster bed, and Percival purred proudly.

"And at your time of life!" said the Catlady.

Then she realized that though her mother if still alive would have been in her nineties, the cat she had become was young. What's more, when the coming kittens were born to Percival and Florence (to Mama and Papa, that is to say), they would be, strictly speaking, her own little brothers and sisters!

She hurried downstairs to the kitchens. "Mary! Mary!" she cried. "She is going to have kittens!"

"Who, Miss Muriel?"

In the nick of time the Catlady stopped herself from replying "My Mama".

"My Florence!" she said. "I had thought she was just putting on too much weight but now I see what it is!"

More kittens, thought Mary, as if there weren't enough cats about the place already. Maybe this is the moment to suggest cutting down the numbers.

"Wouldn't it be a good idea to get rid of a few of your cats, Miss Muriel?" she asked.

"Get rid of them?"

"Yes. Find good homes for them."

"But how?"

"I could put an advertisement in the local paper."

A few days later readers of the *Dummerset Chronicle* saw the following notice:

... without a the stone. ... TICE on the field ... oin is not sh in a nold ... eu forseven on this. The ill be placed vale instrict iance with foremention ...

NUMBER OF CATS AND KITTENS, FREE TO GOOD HOMES. Apply Mary Nutt, Ponsonby Place, Dumpton Muddicorum, Dummerset.

FARM LAND FOR SALE

... havin in son causin intra effor ... PC INS call and inst eve bet

"You don't have to do anything, Miss Muriel," Mary said. "I give you my word I'll make sure they go to good homes."

In the next few weeks a lot of people came walking, cycling, or riding up the drive to

Ponsonby Place. Some owned a cat but fancied having another, some had lost their cat and wanted to replace it, some had never owned a cat before but were attracted by that one word FREE. Many were just curious and keen to take this chance to see the Catlady in her own home.

Such was the demand that soon Mary was having to turn people away. She pinned a notice on the front door that said:

"All those that have gone have got good homes, I'm sure, Miss Muriel," she said to the Catlady, who was sitting in an armchair in the drawing-room, with the Queen of the United Kingdom on her lap, reading a book called *The Care of Cats*.

"Well done, Mary dear," the Catlady said. "Though I shall miss them all very much."

Let's hope, she thought, that my Florence (Mama, that is) has a lot of kittens.

As though to compensate for the losses, Florence gave birth the very next day, on the fine silken bedspread of the four-poster in the bedroom of the Catlady's late parents.

"Oh Mama!" breathed Muriel Ponsonby as she bent over the two new-born kittens. One was a tortoiseshell like the mother, the other white like the father who sat nearby, purring with pride.

The Catlady had been an only child, but now she thought – I have a baby brother and a baby sister!

"Oh Papa," she said, "what shall we call them?" But of course Percival merely replied "Mu".

"I'll ask Mary," said the Catlady and she followed Vicky (who always liked to lead the way) down to the kitchens.

If only Mary knew, she thought as she told the good tidings, that these two new kittens are the children of my dear Mama and Papa, so that now I have the brother and the sister I never had as a child.

"Come up and see them," she said, and then as they stood looking down she said, "What shall we call them? Why don't you choose, Mary Nutt?"

Mary laughed.

"We could call them after some sort of nut!" she said.

"What a good idea," said the Catlady. "Let's see now, there's walnut and peanut . . ."

". . . and chestnut and beechnut and groundnut . . ."

". . . and coconut and hazelnut," said the Catlady.

"Hazel," said Mary. "That would be a nice name for the little female, wouldn't it?"

"Oh yes!" said the Catlady. "But what about the little tom?"

"Coco, Miss Muriel," said Mary. "Short for coconut."

"I like it!" cried the Catlady.

My sister Hazel, she thought, and my brother

Coco. What fun! How lucky I am to believe in reincarnation. It would be nice for Mary to believe too. Just think – her father for instance, Arthur, I think he was called, suppose he's now a boy or a horse perhaps or a dog or maybe even something as small as a mouse. No, not a mouse, they don't live long enough, he'd have gone into yet another body by now, dead of old age or, worse, killed by a cat. Just think, if dear Papa had eaten Arthur Nutt!"

But it might help Mary, she said to herself, to know that I at least believe that her father is not dead and gone. His body might be buried on some

113

South African battlefield, but his personality, his spirit, his soul, call it what you like, has been reincarnated, has entered some other body. Maybe I should try to explain it to her.

"Mary dear, tell me, is it very painful for you to talk of your parents?"

"Painful?" replied Mary. "Yes, it will always be painful. But they've gone. I just have to accept that."

"Gone," said the Catlady. "Gone where?"

"To Heaven, I suppose. They were good people."

"Have you ever thought," asked the Catlady, "that they might have been reincarnated?"

"What does that mean?"

"That they might have been reborn, in some other shape or form?"

"Oh, I don't think I could believe in that," Mary said.

"I do," said the Catlady.

Mary Nutt looked at her employer, the elderly green-eyed Catlady, grey hair tied back as usual. She's aged quite a bit in the time I've lived here, she thought, rather bent, a bit unsteady on her feet, but her mind is still clear, I think. Or rather, I thought. But this reincarnation thing!

"Do you mean," Mary asked, "that you believe you were someone else in a previous life?"

"Someone. Or perhaps somebody. I wasn't necessarily human."

"You could have been an animal?"

"Yes, indeed. I may be one in the future, when my heart stops beating. I don't expect you to believe in the idea, Mary, but I thought it might be a comfort to you to know that I am sure your mother and father are still enjoying lives of some sort. As indeed my dear Mama and Papa are."

"Your mother and father?"

"At this moment they are in their old bedroom, resting upon their four-poster bed, while my brother and sister play on the floor."

"I don't understand," said Mary.

"Percival and Florence. My father and mother."

"Those were their names?"

"Those are their names. New forms they may have acquired, but I know without a shadow of a doubt who they were before they became cats. Just as I am absolutely certain about Vicky here. She was born at twenty past four on the afternoon of January 22nd 1901, the very instant that the last breath left her previous body."

"Whose body was that?" Mary asked.

"Vicky, as I most disrespectfully call her, is in fact Victoria, Queen of the United Kingdom and Empress of India," said the Catlady.

She picked up the stout ginger cat and began, with great deference, to stroke her. "So now you know, Mary," she said. "Vicky here is the late great Queen Victoria."

Did I tell myself her mind was clear, Mary thought. She's barmy.

CHAPTER FIVE

The shopkeepers in Dumpton Muddicorum had always thought Miss Ponsonby a bit mad. You'd have to be, they said, to keep as many cats (and spend as much money on their food) as the Catlady does.

Nonetheless they were still rather fond of her. She was always smiling, always polite. "She may be a bit strange," they said amongst themselves, "but she's a proper lady."

Of course they knew nothing of her belief in reincarnation, but had commented, first, on her kindness in giving away some of her cats ("Free," they said. "She never asked for a penny"), and, secondly, on the fact that the years seemed to be telling on her. Riding her bicycle was patently becoming a big effort.

"Good job she's got that nice young girl living with her, what's her name . . . Mary . . . Mary Nutt, that's it," they said. They were not surprised when Mary appeared in the village one day, riding the Catlady's tall black bicycle, to do the shopping. They each made regular enquiries of Mary as to how Miss Ponsonby was getting on.

One day Mary came back from the village to find the Catlady standing at the front door, leaning on the walking-stick that she now always used, and looking, Mary could see, very worried.

"What is it, Miss Muriel?" Mary asked before beginning to unload the shopping from the big wicker basket on the handle-bars. "What's the matter?"

"Oh Mary!" cried the Catlady. "It's my brother!"

"Your brother?"

"Yes, Coco. I can't find him anywhere. I've asked Mama and Papa and my sister Hazel where Coco has gone but of course they couldn't tell me. Could he have been stolen, d'you think, or run away? I've searched the house but I can't find him."

"He must be some-where about," Mary said. "I'll just unload this shopping and then I'll make you a nice cup of tea. I'll find him, don't you worry."

In fact the white kitten Coco, adventurous as most boys are, had decided to do some exploring.

In the master bedroom of Ponsonby Place there was a large fireplace, once used to keep Sir Percival and Lady Ponsonby warm on winter nights. When Coco was alone in the room, he began to nose around it. Looking up, he saw the sky through the chimney stack. He also saw that there were little stone steps on the walls of the chimney, steps up which, long ago, children had been sent to sweep down the soot with bags full of goose-feathers. Coco began to climb. As he did so, the soot began to fall and he became covered in the stuff. It got in his eyes and his nose and his mouth, and he became very fright-ened. He did not know whether to go on up or to come back down or what to do. He sat on one of the steps, mewing pitifully for his mother.

He was there, of course, when the Catlady was searching for him, but her hearing was too poor to catch his muffled cries and her eyesight not sharp enough to notice the fallen soot in the fire-place.

But Mary, when she began to search, both heard the kitten and saw the sootfall. Cautiously she peered up the chimney and saw the crouching figure of the tiny adventurer.

"Oh Coco!" she called. "However are you going

to get out of there?" The answer was immediate.

Perhaps it was the sight of her face, perhaps the sound of her voice, perhaps he simply lost his footing, but the next minute Coco came tumbling down into the fireplace.

Mary, by now very sooty herself, carried him 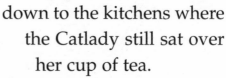 down to the kitchens where the Catlady still sat over her cup of tea.

"Here he is!" she said.

"But Mary," the Catlady cried, peering through her spectacles, "my brother Coco is a white kitten, like Papa, and that one is coal-black."

"Coal-black's about right," Mary said, and she set about cleaning the unhappy Coco, while on the floor below the sink, his parents watched and waited.

"Whatever has the boy been doing?" Percival asked his wife.

"Went up the chimney by the look of it," replied Florence.

"Why?"

"I've no idea, Percival. Boys will be boys."

The Colonel looked smug. "Chip off the old

block," he said rather proudly. "I was always an adventurous lad."

But Coco was not the only adventurous one. A few days later it was Hazel who went missing. Coco had gone up. She went down.

Below the ground floor of Ponsonby Place were the cellars, though the door to them was nowadays seldom opened. The flight of steps that led down to the racks where Colonel Sir Percival Ponsonby had kept his wine (when he was a man) were very steep, and the Catlady hadn't been down there for years.

But recently Mary had taken to using the racks for storing things and on this particular day she had gone down to fetch some cloths and some shoe-polish. Unbeknownst to her, someone else slipped down too.

Mary came back up the steep steps and shut the cellar door. She got out Miss Ponsonby's bicycle and set off to do the shopping.

When she returned, she found, once again, the Catlady standing at the front door, leaning on her walking-stick. This time, however, she looked delighted, her old face wreathed in smiles.

"Oh Mary!" she cried. "It's my sister!"

"Your sister?"

"Yes, Hazel. I lost her. I couldn't find her anywhere. But someone else did find her!"

"Who?"

The Catlady pointed down at Vicky, who was sitting at her feet, looking extremely smug.

"Her Most Gracious Majesty found her," said the

Catlady. "How Hazel got there I do not know, but she was in the cellars. Somehow she'd been shut in there."

"Oh," said Mary.

"I was getting so worried," the Catlady said. "I looked everywhere, I listened everywhere, but as I think you know, these days neither my sight nor my hearing are what they used to be. I asked Papa and Mama but they didn't seem to understand. And then something extraordinary

happened, Mary. Vicky came up to me and put a paw on my stocking – something she has never done before – and then turned and walked away, stopping and looking back every so often. Clearly she wanted me to follow her, so I did. She led me to the cellar door and when I opened it, there was my poor sister sitting on the steps. How glad I was to see her, and so were Papa and Mama and Coco. And how grateful I am to Her Majesty!"

The Catlady bent down and, very respectfully, stroked Vicky's fat ginger back.

"Thank you, Ma'am, thank you so much," she said, and Vicky purred loudly.

Percival and Florence of course discussed this latest event in their own language.

"How in the world did the girl come to be shut in the cellars?" the Colonel asked his wife.

At that moment, Vicky came into the master bedroom. She was the only cat in the house to be allowed in that room, though normally she spent her days and nights on the Catlady's bed.

Percival and Florence, who had both been lying on the carpet, sprang up, and Percival stood rigidly to attention like the soldier he had once been.

He waited for Vicky to speak (it was customary among all the cats not to address the Queen first but to wait to be spoken to).

"Well, Colonel," Vicky said, "I trust that your daughter is none the worse for this latest incident?"

"She came to no harm, Your Majesty," Percival

replied, "but she might have been imprisoned for a long time had it not been for your skill in finding her, Ma'am. My wife and I are truly grateful."

"It was nothing," Vicky said. "We happened to be passing the cellar door and we heard the child mewing. 'Kittens should be seen and not heard' as the saying goes, but on this occasion it was fortunate that the child cried out."

"And that Your Majesty's hearing is so sharp," said Florence.

"All our five senses are in perfect working order," said Vicky imperiously and she waddled regally out of the room.

CHAPTER SIX

Probably on account of the Catlady's strangely respectful treatment of Vicky, Mary Nutt began, despite herself, to think quite a lot about this strange idea of reincarnation.

In the Catlady's library she first consulted an encyclopaedia. "This belief", she read, "is fundamental to the Hindu and Buddhist concepts of the world."

So millions of people believe in it, she thought.

They can't all be barmy. Perhaps Miss Muriel isn't, either.

Reincarnation, she read, accounts for the differences in the character of individuals because of what each had once been. So was the fact that Vicky was short and tubby and bossy and that the other cats always let her eat first and seemed to be very respectful towards her – was that all because this ginger cat had once been Queen of England? Rubbish, one part of her said.

Millions believe in it, said another. Of course it would be a comfort to me to be able to believe that my mother and father are alive again, in some shape or form. If only I could, she thought.

I wonder what form Miss Muriel believes she will assume, when she dies? Which may not be all that long, she thought. She's aged a great deal in the years that I've been here.

For some time now the Catlady had not come

down for breakfast. She ate very little anyway, and Mary, seeing how frail she was becoming, persuaded her to have a tray with a cup of tea and some toast and marmalade brought up to her bedroom.

One morning Mary knocked as usual and took in the tray.

"Shall I pour for you both, Miss Muriel?" she asked.

"Please, Mary dear."

So she saw to the Catlady's tea and then, as usual, filled a saucer with milk and put it on the floor for Vicky.

"How are we today, Miss Muriel?" she asked.

"A little tired. I'm not getting any younger, I fear."

"You stay in bed," Mary said. "I can bring you some lunch up later."

You're really looking very old now, she

thought. But not unhappy. Maybe because of this belief of yours that when you die, you'll start again as someone or something else.

"I've been thinking quite a lot," she said, "about what you said to me some time ago. About being reborn, in another body."

"I shall be," said the Catlady firmly.

It still seems odd that she's so sure, Mary thought.

The Catlady did not get up at all that day, saying that she did not have the energy. It was the same all that week, a week that by chance contained two bereavements for Muriel Ponsonby. The cat that had once been her Uncle Walter died, and then her old schoolfriend Margaret Maitland.

"Both cats were very old though, weren't they?" Mary said in an effort to console her friend.

"As I am," said the Catlady.

"Anyway," said Mary, "it's nice for you to think they will both be reborn, isn't it?"

"As I shall be," said the Catlady.

What am I saying, Mary asked herself. I'm barmy too.

She could not make up her mind whether the

Catlady was just tired or whether she was ill. And if so, how ill? Should I call the doctor, she thought?

What decided her was a request that the Catlady made.

"Mary dear," she said. "Would you fetch Percival and Florence and Coco and Hazel? I should like to say goodbye to them."

When Mary had done so, she telephoned the doctor. He came and examined the old lady, and then he took Mary aside and said to her, "I'm afraid Miss Ponsonby is very ill. To be honest with you, my dear, I don't hold out much hope."

"She's dying, you mean?" Mary asked.

"I fear so."

Shall I tell him about Miss Muriel's beliefs, she thought? No, he'll think I'm mad as well as her. The next morning Mary Nutt woke early and dressed. As she went downstairs from her bedroom in what had been the servants' quarters and made her way to the kitchen, she noticed something odd. There was not a cat to be seen, anywhere.

She was about to put a kettle on to make tea when one cat walked in through the kitchen door.

It was Vicky, who stared up at Mary with her customary grumpy look and made a noise which meant, Mary had no doubt, "Follow me".

Up the stairs
went Vicky, Mary
at her heels, and
in through the
open door of
the Catlady's
bedroom.

Dick King-Smith

On the floor, in a rough circle around the bed, were sitting all the other cats of Ponsonby Place: Percival and Florence and their children, Rupert and Madeleine, the newly widowed Aunt Beatrice, Ethel and Edith, and a number of others. All sat quite still, gazing up at the bed, on which the Catlady lay stretched and still. On her face was a gentle smile.

Mary picked up a hand. It was icy cold. "Oh Miss Muriel," she whispered. "Who or what are you now?"

Chapter Seven

The vicar was afraid that the funeral of the late Miss Muriel Ponsonby might be very poorly attended. Her mother and father were long dead, he knew (though he did not know that they, and other relatives, still lived, in different shape, in Ponsonby Place). The only mourner he expected to see was Mary Nutt.

What a pity, he thought, that the daughter of Colonel Sir Percival Ponsonby and

Lady Ponsonby, of Ponsonby Place, one of the finest old houses in Dummerset, should go to

her grave almost unmourned.

In fact, on the day when the Catlady was buried, the vicar's church was jam-packed.

All the villagers of Dumpton Muddicorum and all the tradesmen and a number of other people in the neighbourhood who owned cats that had once belonged to Muriel, all of these turned up to pay their respects. All the Catlady's oddities were forgotten and only her kindness and cheerfulness remembered.

"She was a funny one," they said, "but there was something ever so nice about her. Always so polite too."

"Yes and she was a kind lady, taking in Mary Nutt like she did."

Nor were humans the only mourners. At the back of the church, behind the rearmost pews, sat a silent line of cats.

*

When it was all over, Mary ate her tea in the kitchen while on the floor the various cats ate theirs (Vicky first, of course). What's to become of me, she thought. I can't stay here now that Miss Muriel's dead. The house will be sold, I suppose.

"I don't know," she said to the cats. "I just don't know."

But a week later, she did.

She was summoned to the offices of the

Catlady's solicitor in a nearby town, to be told some astonishing news.

"This, Miss Nutt," said the solicitor, "is a copy of the will of Miss Muriel Ponsonby. As you know, she had no remaining family, no one for whose benefit Ponsonby Place might be sold. She therefore decided that she would leave the house to the RSPC."

"RSPC?" asked Mary.

"The Royal Society for the Protection of Cats.

So that the charity might use Ponsonby Place as its national headquarters. More, the will states that, because of your loyal service to her and her deep affection for you, you should continue to live there, rent-free, for as long as you wish. I am delighted to tell you that Miss Ponsonby has left you a substantial sum of money, to cover your day-to-day expenses and to enable you to employ such help as a housekeeper and a gardener. You are a very fortunate young lady."

Fortunate indeed, thought Mary afterwards. But oh, how I shall miss her! And so will the cats.

Six months later the RSPC had not yet moved in to Ponsonby Place but Mary, with help, was keeping things in apple-pie order. The only change she made was to remove Vicky from the Catlady's bedroom, and Percival and Florence from the master-bedroom, and to shut both bedroom doors.

"You'll just have to find other rooms to sleep in," she said to them all, and fat ginger Vicky

gave her a look that said plainly "We are not amused".

Six months to the day from the death of the Catlady, Mary saw a strange cat come walking

up the drive towards the house, in a very confident way, as though it knew just what it was about.

It was a grey cat, about six months old, Mary guessed, with a sharp face and green eyes and rather pointed ears. A female, she was sure, by the look of it.

It walked straight up to her and began to rub itself against her legs, purring very loudly indeed. Then it walked straight in through the front door. Mary followed.

The stranger set off up the stairs and along the landing, to the now closed door of the bedroom of the Late Muriel Ponsonby. Standing on its hindlegs, it reached up with a forepaw

as though trying to turn the door-handle.

Mystified, Mary opened the door for it, and it ran into the room and leaped upon the bed. It lay there, ears pricked, its green eyes staring into hers with a look that told Mary Nutt exactly what had happened, something that, up to this moment, she had never quite been able to believe possible.

This strange green-eyed grey cat, this lady cat was . . . the Catlady!

"Oh Miss Muriel!" Mary breathed. "You're back!"

THE END

Dick King~Smith

The
Guard Dog

Illustrated by Jocelyn Wild

CHAPTER ONE

There were six puppies in the window of the pet shop. People who know about dogs would have easily recognized their breeds. There was a Labrador, a springer spaniel, an Old English sheepdog, a poodle and a pug.

But even the most expert dog-fancier

couldn't have put a name to the sixth
one. In fact, most of those who stopped
to look in the pet-shop window either
didn't notice it (because it was so

extremely small) or thought it was a rough-haired guinea-pig (which it resembled in size and shape) that had got into the wrong pen.

"What on earth is that?" the rest had said to one another when the sixth puppy was first put in with them. "Looks like something the cat dragged in!" And they sniggered amongst themselves.

"I say!" said the Old English sheepdog puppy loudly. "What *are* you?"

The newcomer wagged a tail the length of a pencil-stub.

"I'm a dog," it said in an extremely small voice.

The pug snorted.

"You could have fooled me," said the poodle.

"Do you mean," said the Labrador, "that you're a dog, as opposed to a bitch?"

"Well, yes."

"But what sort of dog?" asked the springer spaniel.

"How d'you mean, what sort?"

The pug snorted again, and then they all started barking questions.

"What breed are you?"

"What variety of dog?"

"Why are you so small?"

"Why are you so hairy?"

"Are you registered with the Kennel Club?"

"How many champions have you in your pedigree?"

"Pedigree?" said the sixth puppy. "What's a pedigree?

There was a stunned silence, broken at last by a positive volley of snorts.

"Pshaw!" said the pug. "He's a mongrel!"

At that they all turned their backs and began to talk among themselves.

"I say!" said the Labrador. "D'you know what I'm going to be when I grow up?"

"A gun-dog, I bet," said the springer spaniel, "like me. I'm going to be a gun-dog and go out with my master and bring back the pheasants he shoots."

"No," said the Labrador, "as a matter of fact I'm not. I'm going to be a guide-dog for the blind. A much more worthwhile job."

"No more worthwhile than mine," said the Old English sheepdog. "I'm going to work sheep. I'll be galloping about all over the countryside . . ."

". . . getting filthy dirty," interrupted the poodle, "while I'm having my coat shampooed and specially trimmed and clipped, and a silk ribbon tied in my topknot. I'm going to be a show-dog and win masses of prizes."

The pug snorted.

"What about you?" barked the others. "You haven't said what you're going to be when you grow up."

"I am going to be a lap-dog," said the pug loftily. "I shall be thoroughly spoiled and eat nothing but chicken and steak, and the only exercise I shall take will be to walk to my food-dish. Pshaw!"

"What about me?" said
that extremely small voice.
"You haven't asked me what
I'm going to be when I grow up."

The Labrador yawned.

"Oh, all right," it said. "Tell us if you must."

"I," said the sixth puppy proudly, "am going to be a guard-dog."

At this the others began to roll helplessly about, yapping and yelping and snorting with glee.

"A guard-dog!" they cried.

"Mind your ankles, burglars!"

"He's not tall enough to reach their ankles!"

"If he did, those little teeth would only tickle them!"

"Perhaps his bark is worse than his bite!"

"It is!" said the sixth puppy. "Listen!"

Then, out of his hairy little mouth came the most awful noise you can possibly imagine. It was a loud noise, a very very loud noise for such a tiny animal, but its volume was nothing like as awful as its tone.

Think of these sounds: chalk scraping on a blackboard, a wet finger squeaking on a window-pane, a hacksaw cutting through metal, rusty door-hinges creaking, an angry baby screaming, and throw in the horribly bubbly sound of someone with a really nasty cough. Mix them all up together and there you have the noise that the sixth puppy made.

It was a dreadful noise, a revolting disgusting jarring vulgar noise, and it set all the creatures in the pet shop fluttering and scuttering about in panic. As for the other puppies, they bunched

together as far away as they could get,
their hackles raised, their lips wrinkled
in loathing.

At last, after what seemed an age, the

sixth puppy stopped. Head on one side, he wagged his pencil-stub tail.

"You see," he said happily in his usual extremely small voice. "I can make quite a rumpus when I really try."

CHAPTER TWO

"Nobody will buy him," said the other puppies later. "That's for sure."

"What a racket!" said the sheepdog.

"It made me feel quite ill!" said the gun-dog.

"A really common noise!" said the guide-dog.

"Made by a really common animal!" said the show-dog.

"Pshaw!" said the lap-dog.

They all stared balefully at the guard-dog.

"The sooner he's sold, the better," they said.

And that afternoon, he was.

Into the pet shop walked a tall lady with a face that looked as though it had a bad smell under its nose, and a small fat girl.

"I am looking for a puppy," said the lady to the shopkeeper, "for my daughter. I know nothing about dogs. Which of these would you recommend?"

All the puppies lolloped forward to the inner wire of the pen, whining and wagging and generally looking as irresistible as puppies do. All, that is, except the guard-dog. He sat alone, small and silent. He was not exactly sulking – that was not in his nature – but he still felt very hurt.

"Nobody will buy him. That's for sure," they had said.

He resigned himself to life in a pet shop.

The shopkeeper was busy explaining the various virtues of the five pedigree puppies when the fat child, who was standing, sucking her thumb, took it out with a plop.

She pointed at the guard-dog.

"Want that one," she said.

"Oh, that's just a mongrel puppy, dear," said the shopkeeper. "I expect Mummy would prefer . . ."

"Want that one."

"But, darling . . ."

The small fat girl stamped her small fat foot. She frowned horribly. She hunched her shoulders. With a movement that was as sudden as it was decisive, she jammed her thumb

back in her small fat mouth.

"She wants that one," said her mother.

By the end of that day, the guard-dog was feeling pretty pleased with life.

To be sure, there were things about his new owners that he did not quite understand. It seemed, for example, that simple pleasures like chewing carpets and the bottom edges of curtains drove

the lady into what he considered a quite unreasonable rage, and as for the child, she was temperamental, he thought, to say the least.

Though at first she had seemed willing to play with him, she soon began to complain that his teeth were too sharp or his claws too scratchy or his tongue too slobbery, and had made a ridiculous fuss over a doll which had sported a fine head of hair and was now bald.

Strange creatures, he thought that night when at last all was quiet, but I mustn't grumble. I'm warm and well-fed and this seems a very fine house for a guard-dog to guard. Which reminds me – it's time I was off on my rounds.

Ears cocked, nose a-quiver, he pattered off on a tour of the downstairs rooms.

His patrol over, he settled down in a basket in the kitchen. There was plain evidence that he had done his duty. In the centre of the drawing-room, for example, there was a fine white fleecy rug, and in the centre of the rug was a bright yellow pool. In other rooms there were other messes.

Comfortable now, the guard-dog closed his extremely small eyes. It had been a tiring day, and he was just drifting off to sleep when suddenly, outside the kitchen door, he heard a stealthy sound! He leaped to his feet.

CHAPTER THREE

Afterwards the family could not understand why their cat would never again enter the house, but lived, timidly, in the garden shed. They did not know that its nerves had been shattered by the simple act of pressing against the cat-flap, something it had done every

day of its life. This had resulted instantly in a noise that sounded to its horrified ears like a number of cats being scrunched up in a giant mincer. Upstairs, the fat child woke screaming, and soon her mother came rushing down those stairs and stepped in something unusual at the bottom.

Even then the guard-dog might still have had a house to guard (for it was difficult for them to believe that so little a creature was capable of making so ghastly a noise), if only he had kept his mouth shut the next morning.

But he stuck to his task, challenging everything that seemed to him a threat to the territory which it was his duty to protect. Quite early, at the sound of whistling and the chink of bottles outside the door, he woke his owners

once more. And no sooner had they taken the milk in than the postman knocked, and they actually saw the guard-dog in action.

Happily unaware of the effect of his voice upon the human ear, and mindful only of his role – to give warning of the approach of strangers – the guard-dog kept it up all morning.

The cleaning woman (who found a great deal of cleaning to do), the paper boy, the electricity man come to read the meter, and a door-to-door salesman were each in turn greeted by the dreadful medley of sounds that emerged, full blast, from the guard-dog's tiny throat. Last came a collector for the RSPCA, the rattle of whose tin inspired the guard-dog to his loudest, longest and most furious outburst.

"RSPCA?" screamed his distracted

owner. "What about a society for the prevention of cruelty to people?" And at midday, as she unscrewed the

Aspirin bottle, she said to her daughter, "I'm sorry, darling, but I cannot stand that row a moment longer. It'll have to go. Will you be very upset?"

The small fat girl, her eyes fixed malevolently upon the guard-dog, did not even bother to remove her thumb from her mouth. She merely shook her head, violently.

*

That afternoon the guard-dog found himself, to his surprise, in a very different kind of home – the Dogs' Home. He could not make out what had gone wrong. What were guard-dogs meant to do if not guard? He had only done his duty, but all he had received so far had been angry looks and angry words before finally they bundled him into their car, and drove him to a strange place full of strange dogs and left him.

From the kennel he had been given, Number 25, he looked round him. There was every sort of dog in the kennel block, young and old, handsome and ugly, large and small (though none remotely as small as he). Why were they all there?

"Why are we all here?" he asked the dog directly opposite him, a sad-looking

animal with long droopy ears and a long
droopy face.

"Because," said the dog dolefully, "we
are all failures."

I don't get it, thought the guard-dog.
My job is to give warning of the approach
of strangers. I've never yet failed in that.

"I don't think I'm a failure," he said.

"Well, you're certainly not a success," said the long-faced dog, "or you wouldn't be here. All of us are here because our owners couldn't stand us any longer."

"But we'll get new owners, won't we?"

"Possibly. It depends."

"Depends on what?"

"On whether you take someone's fancy. You just have to do whatever you're best at. Me, I'm best at looking sad. Some people like that."

In the days that followed, many people in search of a suitable pet came to inspect the twenty or so current inmates of the

Dogs' Home; and when they came to the end of the range of kennels and found the smallest inhabitant, they would without exception break into smiles at the sight of such a charming little scrap.

Without exception, however, they were treated to the dreadful spectacle of the guard-dog doing what he was best at. And without exception the smiles vanished, to be replaced by looks of horror as they turned away with their hands clapped to their ears.

By the time the guard-dog had been in the Dogs' Home for a week, most of the animals had gone happily (or in the case of the long-faced dog, sadly) away with new owners, and there were newcomers in most of the kennels.

By the thirteenth day, there was only one dog left of those who had been there when he was admitted. This was his next-door neighbour, an old and rather smelly terrier.

The guard-dog's attempts to make conversation with it had always thus far been met with a surly growl, so he was quite surprised when he was suddenly addressed.

"You bin in 'ere thirteen days, littl'un, an't you?" said the terrier.

"Oh," said the guard-dog, "have I?"

"Ar. You come in day after I. 'Tis my fourteenth day."

"Oh well," said the guard-dog, "try not to worry. I'm sure you'll soon be gone."

"Ar," said the terrier. "I shall. Today."

"But how can you know that? How can you know that someone's going to take you away today?"

"Fourteen days is the limit, littl'un. They don't keep you no longer than that."

"Why, what do they do with you then?"

"An't nobody told you?"

"No."

"Ar well," said the old terrier. "'Tis all right for us old uns, 'tis time to go. I shan't be sorry. You don't feel nothing, they do say. But 'tis a shame for a nipper like you."

"I don't understand," said the guard-dog. "What are you trying to tell me?" But though he kept on asking, the old dog only growled at him, and then lay silent, staring blankly out of its kennel. Later, a man in a white coat came and led it gently away.

Chapter Four

"Oh, thanks," said the manager of the Dogs' Home, when one of his kennelmaids brought in his cup of coffee at eleven o'clock next morning. He looked up from his record book.

"Shame about the little titchy one in Number twenty-five," he said.

"You don't mean . . . ?" said the kennelmaid.

"'Fraid so. If things had been slack we could have kept him longer, but the way dogs are pouring in, we must keep to the two-week rule. He's one for the vet today."

"Oh dear," said the kennelmaid. "He's such a lovely little fellow. Dozens of people fell for him, until . . ."

". . . until he opened his mouth," said the manager. "I know. It's a pity, but you can't blame them. In all my long experience of every sort of dog, I've never come across one with such a dreadful voice. Nobody could possibly live with that; though, talk about burglar alarms – any burglar would run a mile if he heard that hullabaloo. And you wouldn't need to dial nine-nine-nine – they'd hear it at the nearest police station easy."

*

The guard-dog ate a hearty breakfast, and was a little surprised when the kennelmaid came to clean out his run, at the fuss she made of him. She cuddled and stroked and kissed him as if she would never see him again.

Then he remembered what the smelly old terrier had said. This is my fourteenth day, he thought. Great! Someone will pick me out today! He sat, waiting for the time when the public were admitted, determined that today of all days he would leave no-one in any doubt as to the quality of his greatest asset. Other guard-dogs, he supposed, might act in other ways, by looking large and fierce (which he could not) or by leaping up and planting their feet on the shoulders of burglars and suchlike and knocking them flat (which he most certainly could not). He had only his voice, and when the door to the kennel block opened, he let rip, fortissimo.

No-one even got to smiling at him that morning. Everybody kept as far away as possible from the dreadful sounds issuing from Number 25, and concentrated upon the other inmates. The guard-dog was left strictly alone.

When at last the batch of would-be owners had left, some with new companions, some empty-handed, all mightily relieved to reach the comparative peace and quiet of the busy roaring street outside, the guard-dog sat silent once more. There was a puzzled look on his extremely small and hairy face.

Can't understand it, he thought. Nobody seems to want a decent guard-dog. But if fourteen days was the limit, then they'd jolly well have to find him somewhere to go today. Perhaps the man in the white coat would take him too – he'd seemed a nice sort of chap.

He watched the door to the kennel block.

It was not the man in the white coat who came in but the kennelmaid with a man with white hair, who walked with a stick with a rubber tip to it.

"Would you like

me to come round with you?" the kennelmaid said, but he did not answer, so she went away and left him alone.

The old man walked slowly along the row of kennels, looking carefully into each with sharp blue eyes. At last he came to Number 25.

Outside the door, the kennelmaid stood listening, her fingers tightly crossed. But then she heard that fearful noise start up and shook her head sadly.

She went back into the kennel block to

find the old man squatting on his heels. There was a grin on his face as he looked, apparently totally unmoved, at the howling bawling yowling squalling guard-dog. He levered himself to his feet.

"I'll have this little fellow," he said firmly. "He's the boy for me."

"Oh good!" cried the kennelmaid. "He's lovely, don't you think?" But the old man did not answer.

He did not reply later either, when he had paid for the guard-dog and the kennelmaid said, "Would you like a box to carry him in?" And in answer to the manager's question, "What are you going to call him?" he only said, "Good afternoon."

Light suddenly dawned on the manager of the Dogs' Home. He stood directly in front of the guard-dog's new owner so as to be sure of catching his eye, and said deliberately, in a normal tone, "That's some dog you've got there. The worst voice in the world!"

The old man put his hand up to his ear.

"Sorry?" he said. "Didn't catch that. I'm as deaf as a post and I can't be bothered with those hearing-aid things – never been able to get on with them. What did you say?"

"That's some dog you've got there. The best choice in the world!" said the manager very loudly.

The white-haired old man only smiled, leaning on his stick with one hand and cradling his purchase in the other.

The manager shouted as loudly as he could, "He's a dear little chappie!"

"See that he's really happy?" said the old man. "Of course I will, you needn't worry about that. We'll be as happy as two peas in a pod."

He fondled the puppy's extremely small hairy ears.

"Funny," he said. "I fell for him though he wasn't actually what I was looking for. I live all on my own, you see, so really it would have been more sensible to get a guard-dog.

THE END

Dick King-Smith

Hairy Hezekiah

Illustrated by John Eastwood

CHAPTER ONE

In a zoo in an English city there lived a camel. Do not think that I am just a liar, when I say his name was Hezekiah. It really was, honestly. He was a Bactrian camel, very big and heavy and covered in a lot of dark brown hair. On his back he carried two large humps. He was well fed and kindly treated, but in one way Hezekiah was different from all the other animals in the zoo.

They had friends to talk to – the lions in the Lion House, the gorillas and chimpanzees in the Ape House, the birds in the Aviary, the monkeys in the Monkey Temple – they all had others of their kind with them or close by. They could roar or scream or whistle or chatter at one another as much as they liked.

But there were no other camels for Hezekiah to make friends with. He was the only one, and he lived in a wire-fenced grass paddock all by himself.

Hezekiah, you will have guessed, was lonely. Visitors to the zoo came and stood by the fence and looked at Hezekiah. They could hear him making deep grumbly noises as he stared out at them through his heavily lashed eyes, but they could not know that he was in fact talking to himself out loud.

He had fallen into this habit because he had no camel friends to speak to, no camel voices to listen to, and, though he didn't suppose the humans could understand him, it comforted him to speak his thoughts to the watching people.

"Wish I had a pal," he often said. "Don't suppose you care but I'm the only camel in the zoo, did you know that?"

Often, in reply to Hezekiah's growling and snorting and the bubbly sounds that he made

through his thick rubbery lips, the visitors made noises too. But of course Hezekiah could not understand what they were saying to him and anyway he couldn't hear much of it because his ears were very hairy inside.

*

One day Hezekiah was standing by the gate into his paddock, staring out through his heavy eyelashes. It was a bitterly cold winter 's day. There were hardly any visitors in the zoo and none at all near him.

He didn't mind the cold a bit as his coat was so thick, but he was more than usually grumpy because he hadn't yet been fed.

"Where's my flipping breakfast?" he growled. "I'm starving. My humps feel all floppy."

Camels store fat in their humps, and if they are really really short of food, the humps shrink in size. Hezekiah wasn't actually starving, of course, just hungry.

When at last he saw his keeper approaching, carrying a bale of hay, he shouted rudely at the man. "Get a move on, slowcoach!" he boomed. "You're late and I'm famished!"

Dick King-Smith

The keeper was a fairly new one who hadn't been at the zoo for long. The only thing he knew about the camel was that he seemed to be a bad-tempered old thing who was always moaning and groaning.

"Keep your hair on, Hezekiah," he said as he slid back the metal bar that kept the gate shut. Now he opened it, threw in the haybale and cut its strings. "There you are, old misery-guts," he called, and he went out again, closing the gate behind him.

Hezekiah tucked into his hay greedily, swallowing it down in great lumps. Like a cow, he would later lie down and chew the cud. When night fell,

226

he got to his feet and, on his huge splayed hooves, lumbered over to the gate of the paddock and stood, as he often did, staring out.

There was no one for him to talk to, for all the visitors had left the zoo, so, as usual, he talked to himself.

"I wish," said Hezekiah, "that I could open this gate. I could have a walk around the place, meet some other animals, make a pal perhaps, even though I'm the only camel in the zoo. I wonder if

I could somehow open the blooming thing. Perhaps it's something to do with that metal bar. Maybe I could shift it."

He lowered his long neck and with his thick blubbery lips he mouthed at the bar. It was stiff and for a while he could not move it. "Easy enough for keepers with fingers and thumbs," he grumbled, "but not for Bactrian camels."

He was on the point of giving up, but then he said to himself, "Oh, come on, Hezekiah, one last go." He gave it one last go and at last the bar slid across and the gate swung open. "Bless my humps!" he said, and walked out.

CHAPTER TWO

The whole of the zoo was dark now, except for lights in a few of the buildings. As Hezekiah made his way towards the nearest one, he heard from within it a deep rolling roar that ended in

a couple of grunts. So he made his entrance through the half-open door into the Lion House.

Now, people cannot understand camel talk and camels can't understand human language. But in one way almost all animals are cleverer than humans, because they can understand one another. To Hezekiah the noise that the lion was making meant "I am the lion, the King of Beasts, and I'm shut up in this horrible cage. Damn and blast!"

The camel made his lumbering way into the dimly lit Lion House and walked along in front of the row of cages. At the sight of him, there was a burst of noise from within them.

"Mum! Mum!" cried some cubs. "Whatever is that thing? Will it hurt us?"

"Of course not," replied a lioness. "First, it can't get into our cage, and second, if it could, I'd kill it and we'd eat it."

"And so would we if only we could get out of our cages," growled several lions.

"But what is it, Mum?" said the cubs. "Ask it," said their mother.

So they did.

Hezekiah stopped and stood, looking into that cage. He didn't like the smell of the lions, so he closed his nostrils as all camels can. He didn't like the sight of them either, with their gleaming teeth and sharp claws, and certainly he didn't like what they had said they wanted to do to him.

But the bars of the cages looked nice and strong, thank goodness, and, in reply to the cubs' question, he said, "Good evening" (for politeness costs nothing). "I am a Bactrian camel."

"Bactrian camel?" said one of the cubs. "What have you got on your back?"

"Two humps."

"What's in them?"

"Fat," said Hezekiah, and all the lions licked their lips.

The biggest of the lions came forward to the front of his cage.

"What are you doing in here?" he asked. "Why aren't you in the Camel House?"

"There isn't one," said Hezekiah. "I live in a paddock."

"Well, why aren't you there?"

"I've escaped," replied Hezekiah, and a huge sigh of envy rippled through the Lion House.

"How did you manage that?" asked the lion, moving closer to the bars. "Oh, and come a little closer, will you? I'm a bit deaf."

I'm not that stupid, thought Hezekiah.

"Tell you some other time," he said, and he turned and hurried out of the Lion House.

He walked along a path to the next building, which was the Ape House, and made his way inside. In the first cage was a big gorilla.

"Good evening," said Hezekiah.

"Is it?" replied the gorilla. "Why?"
"I've escaped."

"All right for some," said the gorilla gloomily.

"Forgive me for asking," said Hezekiah, "but you don't want to eat me, do you?"

233

"Eat you? No, I'm a vegetarian."

"Oh, sorry," said Hezekiah, and he moved on to the next cage, in which were two chimpanzees.

"We heard that," said one.

"And before you ask," said the other, "we are also mostly vegetarians. But now and again we do like a nice bit of monkey-meat."

"But not camel-meat?" wondered Hezekiah.

"What's a camel?" asked the first chimp.

"I am."

"Oh," said the second. "No, thanks." He shouted down to the other chimpanzee cages. "Would any of you chaps like to eat this fellow?" and in reply there were loud screams of laughter.

Hezekiah could still hear the chimpanzees laughing as he made his lumbering way along to the next building in the zoo, which was the Aviary. Inside, almost all the birds were silent, asleep on their perches, though there were some owls who hooted softly at sight of the intruder.

"Who? Who?" they said. "To wit, who?"

"Evening," said the camel. "My name's Hezekiah. I'm a Bactrian camel."

"Hard luck!" said a voice.

Hezekiah peered in and saw a grey parrot staring at him.

"Why do you say that?" he asked.

"Look in the mirror," said the parrot.

I've been threatened, thought Hezekiah, then laughed at, and now insulted. What next?

He made his way out of the Aviary and walked towards the Monkey Temple. This was a big round pit, inside which were flights of circular steps leading up to a stone building in the centre. It had a domed top and looked something like an Eastern temple.

Hezekiah peered over the edge of the wall that surrounded the pit. He could see no monkeys, either on the floor or on the steps. "Good!" he said loudly. "There's no one about to be rude to me."

At the sound of his deep booming voice, a number of little heads popped out of the small windows in the Temple, and he heard a chorus of angry shouts.

"Be quiet!"
"Push off!"
"Sling your hook!"
"Hold your tongue!"
"Shut your trap!"

As he trudged away from the Monkey Temple, Hezekiah began to think that escaping wasn't much fun. "I wanted to make some friends," he said gloomily to the surrounding darkness. "At least nobody was being nasty to me in my own paddock. I wonder what's the next place I shall come to?"

Even as he said this, he saw a single-storey building looming up ahead of him. It seemed to be divided into two halves, each half having a door.

"I wonder who lives here?" he said.

Hezekiah could not read, of course. Had he been able to, he would have seen a notice above each door.

LADIES, one said, and the other GENTS.

Chapter Three

Camels can go a long time without drinking. When they do drink, they can put down an awful lot of water, as much as sixty litres in one go.

As Hezekiah neared the public toilets, his nose told him that there were no animals inside this building, but he could smell water and he realized that he badly needed some.

He'd been so busy earlier grumbling about his food being late that he hadn't had a drink from the trough in his paddock. Now, after what he'd had to put up with in the Lion House and the Ape House and the Aviary and the Monkey Temple, he was very thirsty.

By chance Hezekiah picked the door marked GENTS and somehow squeezed himself through it. To one side was a row of four cubicles, and inside each there stood on the floor a large white basin with a plastic seat on it and a kind of tank above it.

Hezekiah stretched out his long neck to reach one of the basins. It had water in it and he drank greedily till the basin was empty. He did this to each of the four basins in turn till all were empty, but he was still thirsty.

There was a lever sticking out of the tank above each basin, and Hezekiah, out of curiosity, gripped a handle in his mouth and turned it. Immediately

241

there was a rush of water that filled the basin again.

So Hezekiah drained it and turned the handle again and filled the basin and drained it again, on and on, till he was full as much water as he could manage.

Then he squeezed himself out of the GENTS backwards. The wind was cold on that side of the toilet block, so Hezekiah moved round and squeezed himself into the ladies. He lay down on the floor and went to sleep.

He was woken by a loud scream as an early morning cleaner came in and got the shock of her life when she bumped into something large and hairy.

As the cleaner dropped her mop and ran away, Hezekiah got to his feet, gave himself a good shake and looked about him in the growing light. Birds were beginning to sing and monkeys to chatter, and just beyond the public toilets, he could see, were the main gates of the zoo, still closed.

"I've escaped from my poky little paddock," said Hezekiah (not too loudly in case there was someone about), "but I am still a prisoner. If only someone would open those gates. Oh, how I wish they would!"

Maybe there is a special deity that looks after camels, or maybe it was just sheer luck, but at that very moment one of the keepers came out of the lodge beside the gates, and opened them, to be ready in good time for the first of the day's visitors. Even more fortunately, he then went back inside the lodge.

Camels, even great big clumsy Bactrian camels, can move quite fast when they want to. Hezekiah left the shelter of the LADIES and GENTS and was

out through those gates in a flash. His great padded hooves made no sound, and, in a final piece of luck, there was just at that moment no passing traffic on the road outside the zoo. Hezekiah hurried across it into the shelter of some trees.

Looking ahead, he could see green slopes of downland, empty of people at that early hour.

Hezekiah shambled on up them, anxious to get as far as possible from the zoo!

By now the world was waking up, and the

noise of cars and lorries could be heard on the roads below, and then some humans appeared, jogging towards him. Luckily there was a large hollow in the grass nearby, and quickly Hezekiah lay down in it, his neck stretched out flat on the ground, long-lashed eyes and nostrils shut. Had he

had fingers, he would have crossed them. But his luck held and the joggers jogged past without noticing him.

When they had gone, Hezekiah got to his feet and looked about him. Not far away he saw a thick clump of trees.

"Better get in there," he said. "Less chance of

being seen and plenty of leaves to eat. I'll stay there all day and move on when it's dark again. I don't want anyone to see me."

He chomped away at leaves throughout the day until eventually he came to the other side of the clump of trees and found himself on the edge of a garden. In the middle of the garden was a pond where a fountain spurted. Hezekiah wasn't thirsty but he was curious. There didn't seem to be anyone about, so he made his way to the pond.

Inside were a lot of goldfish and they rose to the surface at the sight of the hairy face above them. They opened their mouths in big round "O" shapes and it seemed to the camel that they were all saying, "Who? Who?"

"Actually I'm a Bactrian camel," said Hezekiah. "Don't suppose you've ever seen anything like me before. Can't stop, I'm afraid, in case someone else sees me."

But someone else did see him. It was getting dark by now and in the house at the end of the garden there were two small girls looking out of their bedroom window. They were twins called Josie and Milly, and they very often said the same things at the same time. Now they suddenly saw a large dark shape standing by the goldfish pond.

"Whatever's that?" they said. "Look at its humps, it's a camel," they said, as Hezekiah moved back towards the shelter of the trees.

"Only one place it could have come from," said Josie.

"And that's the zoo," said Milly.

"It's escaped," they said together.

Then they heard their mother's footsteps coming up the stairs.

"Don't let's tell her," said Josie.

"She wouldn't believe us anyway," said Milly. Later Hezekiah made his way on across country, avoiding roads and houses, and when dawn broke the following morning, he found himself in the middle of a large field. A number of strange shapes surrounded him.

They were animals, he could now see, but animals such as he had never set eyes on before. They were quite large, though much smaller than him, and all were black and white in colour. They looked curiously at the camel out of their mild eyes. Hezekiah did not feel threatened by these strange beasts.

"Excuse me," he said. "What are you?"

The animals looked at one another, shaking their heads in bemusement.

"Don't you know?" asked one.

"No."

"We'm Friesians."

"What's a Friesian?"

"A cow."

"What's a cow?" asked the camel. "I've never seen animals like you before."

"We ain't never seen no animals like you before neither," mooed all the cows. "What on earth are you?"

"I'm a Bactrian camel," said Hezekiah.

"Come from Bactria, do 'ee?"

"I suppose so. Like you come from Friesia, I imagine."

Before they say something nasty about me, he thought, I'd better say something nice about them.

"You're very pretty," he said. "Can I ask you something?"

"Go on then," said one of the Friesian cows. "Well, what are those big things between your back legs? Big things with four other things sticking out?"

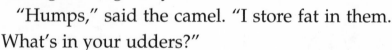

"Udders," they said. "What be them girt things on your back?"

"Humps," said the camel. "I store fat in them. What's in your udders?"

"Milk," they said.

"What for?"

"For people to drink. They do milk us."

People, thought Hezekiah. I don't want them to see me, they'd put me back in the zoo. He decided he'd ask the cows' advice, politely of course.

"I wonder," he said, "if you can help me. You see, I've just escaped from the zoo and I don't want to go back there. I want to find somewhere safe to go, somewhere with lots of space. Do you know of anywhere?"

The cows looked at one another. Then they looked again at the large dark hairy humped figure of the camel. Then one cow came closer to Hezekiah and said, "You'm in luck, my friend. There's a place not far from yur where they do keep all kinds of curious critturs. That's where you do want to go, I reckon."

"Oh," said Hezekiah. "What is this place?"

The cow replied, "'Tis the safari park."

CHAPTER FOUR

"Safari park?" said Hezekiah. "What does that mean?"

"Well," said the cow, "we ain't never bin there, of course, but we do hear tell that 'tis a fine place to live."

"Plenty of room for everyone," said another.

"Bit different from your old zoo, I daresay," said a third.

"How do I get there?"

The whole herd of

Friesians turned to look in one particular direction.

"See them hills in the distance?" they said. "With a good few trees on 'em?"

"Yes," replied Hezekiah.

"That's the edge of the safari park."

"Oh thanks, thanks!" cried Hezekiah. "I'll go on straight away, if you'll all excuse me."

"But you can't get out of this field," they all

said, "till the farmer opens the gate to fetch us in for morning milking."

"Oh I don't need a gate," said the camel. "I'll go out the same way as I came in. Through the hedge."

What a day it was for the farmers of that part of Somerset! Since he had left the Downs in the darkness, Hezekiah had wreaked a trail of havoc through the countryside. Hedges and fences and gates that kept cows and sheep and horses in were no match for the size and strength of the camel. He simply smashed his way through them.

Worse, it was a Sunday, and though farmers work a seven-day week, fifty-two weeks of the year, they do expect to take things a bit easier on a Sunday.

But after Hezekiah burst out again through the

far hedge of the Friesians' field, there was chaos in his wake all through that part of the West Country. Everywhere livestock had taken advantage of the camel's bulldozing passage. Dairy cows, beef cattle, sheep, horses and ponies – all found themselves free to leave their pastures and paddocks and go wherever they pleased.

Farmers can curse as well as most people, but never had there been heard such dreadful cursing as on that Sunday morning. Everyone tried to round up their strays and get them back home and mend the broken gates, the smashed fences, the great camel-sized holes in the hedges.

Dick King-Smith

Hezekiah's Friesian friends were a good example of the fearful confusion for they all went out through the gap that he had made and mingled happily with a neighbouring herd of Ayrshire cows in the next field. It took so long for their angry owners to sort them all out that morning milking did not start till the afternoon.

Hezekiah meanwhile made steady destructive progress towards his goal, crossing, though he did not know it, from Somerset into the county of Wiltshire. He was filled with curiosity about this strange place called a safari park. What would it be like? At last he broke out into a road, a small country lane bordered by trees. Ahead of him was a junction, at which a signpost stood. shortseat, it said.

Hezekiah hesitated. "Is that the way to the safari park?" he asked himself, and then he

heard in the distance the answer to his question. It was a deep rolling roar that ended in a couple of grunts.

CHAPTER FIVE

The great country house of Shortseat was the ancestral home of a noble family. The present Marquess of Basin had inherited the estate on the death of his father, who had turned his well-wooded lands into a safari park. First he introduced lions. Later he brought in other kinds of interesting and attractive animals that would

normally be found behind bars in zoos. But it was the lions of Shortseat that first attracted the public in great numbers.

As well as coming to see the animals, they came to look round the great house, and on that Sunday afternoon it was filled with people. The present Marquess of Basin moved easily among them, chatting with the visitors, most of whom felt honoured to be addressed by such a great nobleman.

This Lord Basin was (like Hezekiah) an extremely hairy person, and he chose to wear very colourful clothes, as though to mark himself out from the common herd.

On this day he was dressed in sky-blue corduroy trousers,

a pink shirt with an emerald-green cravat, and a black velvet jacket lavishly embroidered with gold thread.

At that moment a servant came up to the Marquess. "My Lord," he said, "you are wanted on the telephone."

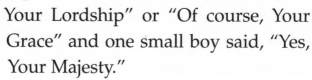

"Will you forgive me?" said Lord Basin to the visitors (for politeness costs nothing). "I fear I must leave you."

"Of course," murmured some, while many others, unsure of how properly to address the nobleman, replied, "Of course, sir" or "Of course, Your Lordship" or "Of course, Your Grace" and one small boy said, "Yes, Your Majesty."

The Marquess of Basin made his way to his study, where his estate manager was waiting, phone in hand.

"It's the police, sir," he said.

"Whatever do they want?" asked Lord Basin. He took the phone. "Hullo?" he said.

"Lord Basin?" said a voice.

"Speaking."

"Sorry to bother you, my Lord, but we were wondering if any of your animals had escaped? It would be a large one by the look of things."

"Escaped?" said the Marquess. "Animals don't escape from Shortseat, they're too happy here. What animals have you found?"

"None, my Lord," replied the policeman, "but we are getting reports of widespread damage in that part of Somerset to the west of you. Everywhere farmers and landowners are reporting broken gates and fences and big holes through hedges, and they suspect that something large and strong may have escaped from Shortseat. There are fears that it might be one of your lions."

"Rubbish!" said Lord Basin loudly. "Lions don't break gates and make holes in hedges. Sounds more like a camel to me."

"Very good, my Lord," said the policeman, and rang off.

Many years ago, when Lord Basin was a boy, his father had taken him on a visit to the very city zoo from which Hezekiah had escaped, and he had ridden on a Bactrian camel.

He'd never forgotten the sensation of sitting between those two great humps as the camel swayed along the paths of the zoo.

When he was a young man, he heard that that

camel had died of old age. When later he inherited Shortseat, he vowed that he would one day have a camel there. But they were very rare. Only a thousand or so still survived in Mongolia's Gobi desert.

"You haven't had any report of anything escaping, have you, John?" said Lord Basin to his manager.

"No, sir."

"Well, whatever 's caused all this damage, it's nothing to do with me."

Even as Lord Basin spoke, Hezekiah was approaching the main gate of the Shortseat Safari Park.

Lord Basin sat back in his office chair, stroking his beard thoughtfully. Maybe the feel of it made him think of hairy creatures.

"Switch on the television, John, please. I want to watch the West Country News."

How I'd love to have a Bactrian camel, he thought, and to his utter amazement the first item on the news was about the escape of a camel from the zoo. It had set off across country, the newscaster said, ending up at Shortseat.

Maybe there is a special deity that looks after marquesses, but at that very moment Hezekiah passed through the gates into Shortseat before the astonished eyes of the gatekeeper and a number of visitors who were about to enter.

With slow steps (for he was now somewhat

hoof-sore) he made his rolling, dignified way, his humps swaying a little, down the long, straight avenue that led to the great house.

Frantically, the gatekeeper telephoned the manager.

Hastily, the manager told the Marquess.

Excitedly, the Marquess made his way through the visitors to the front doors of Shortseat and stood, in his colourful raiment, at the top of the stone steps that led up to the entrance. Behind him, faces peered from every window, witnesses to the arrival of Hezekiah at Shortseat.

They saw the great hairy Lord standing at the top of the steps. They saw the great hairy camel at the bottom.

Hezekiah was very tired now, for he had travelled a long, long way, and he had no intention of trying to climb those steps. Like all camels, he had horny kneepads to rest upon.

So, to the delight of all and in particular of the owner of Shortseat, Hezekiah the Bactrian camel knelt before the Marquess of Basin.

CHAPTER SIX

Later the curator of the zoo rang up. He and the Marquess were old friends, but still there was an edge to his voice as he said, "You've nicked my Bactrian camel!"

"I haven't nicked him," said Lord Basin. "He wasn't invited here, he's just a gatecrasher."

"You can say that again," remarked the

269

curator. "It's going to cost us thousands of pounds to repair the damage."

The Marquess pulled at his beard thoughtfully.

"Look," he said. "I'll pay for the damage."

"Really? That's very good of you."

"On one condition."

"What's that?"

"You let me keep him."

There was a pause, and then the curator said, "It's an idea. But I think we'd need a bit of icing on the cake. What can you offer in return for him?"

"A zebra?"

"Oh no."

"A giraffe?"

"No."

"How about a white tiger?" said Lord Basin.

"It's a deal!"

"Good. By the way, what's the camel's name?"

"Hezekiah."

The Marquess of Basin went to bed that night in a daze of happiness. He was fond of animals in general, but the one that had stuck in his memory all those years was that old Bactrian camel on which he'd ridden in the zoo. And now he actually owned one!

He stroked his beard as he settled himself for sleep. And it's a very hairy beast too, he thought.

*

While Hezekiah had been kneeling below the steps to the front entrance of Shortseat, two of the park rangers had put a rope over his neck, one on either side. They prepared themselves for what they imagined would be quite a tussle when the camel got to his feet. But Hezekiah stood quite quietly, gazing at them with eyes as mild as an old Friesian cow. He did make a lot of rumbling noises, though of course they couldn't under- stand what he was saying.

"Now look, you chaps," he said. "I've come a heck of a long way today and I could do with a good night's sleep."

Which is just what he got, for the rangers decided not to turn him out into one of the enclosures, but to put him, for the time being, in a nice warm old shed, sometimes used to house sick beasts.

After letting him drink his fill from a water

trough, they made him a good bed of straw, and gave him a helping of hay and some interesting roots he'd never seen before. It didn't take long for Hezekiah to decide that he liked mangel-wurzels, and he polished off the lot. Then, with a long sigh of content, he fell into a deep sleep.

He slept so well and dreamlessly that the next thing he knew it was morning. Someone opened the door of the shed and came in. He looked at the man's hairy face and recognized him as the person who had stood at the top of the stairs, dressed in strange clothes.

Lord Basin had risen early and hurried out, still in his night clothes. He wore pyjamas and a dressing-gown and slippers, all very brightly coloured. On his head was a brilliant red woollen nightcap.

"Hezekiah!" he cried.

This was in fact the only word of human language that the camel knew, so often had he heard it. He recognized it as his name. He got to his feet and moved a pace or two towards the Marquess. They looked into each other 's eyes, and

perhaps because each was so hairy, both felt that they were kindred souls and had become – and would always continue to be – best friends.

"I expect you'd like to stretch your legs," said Lord Basin. "It's a bit cramped for you in this old shed. Though you can always come back in here to sleep if you like."

In reply he heard the camel make a number of grunty, growly noises. "Any chance I could stretch my legs?" Hezekiah was saying. "This old shed's not all that big. Though I wouldn't mind coming back in here at night."

The Marquess of Basin put out a hand to his Bactrian camel. Something told him that the animal would not bite his hand, and indeed Hezekiah did not. He merely touched it gently with his thick rubbery lips in a kind of kiss.

CHAPTER SEVEN

After Lord Basin had left the shed to begin the important business of dressing up for the day, the rangers came in to fetch the camel. They led him along one of the park's roads to a very large enclosure, a hundred times bigger than his old zoo paddock.

They opened a gate and let him loose inside, but stayed to watch and make sure there would be no trouble with the other animals in there. They didn't expect any bother, but as well as biting, zebras can kick, and so can ostriches, and so can giraffes.

The rangers watched as the other animals moved towards the camel, curious about this hairy beast that carried two humps on its back.

They formed a circle around the newcomer. Hezekiah stood patiently among them, and the rangers, satisfied, moved off.

There were zebras at the zoo – the camel had seen them from his paddock but he had never before set eyes on a giraffe or an ostrich.

"A very good morning to you all," he said (for politeness costs nothing), "and I hope you'll forgive me for trespassing. It's a pleasure to meet you all and before you ask, I'm a Bactrian camel."

At this, one of the little herd of zebras hee-hawed loudly and one of the three ostriches gave out a deep booming noise. Neither of the two giraffes made a sound.

Then the zebra who had neighed said, "Hope you're a vegetarian, mate."

"Certainly I am. Camels don't eat meat."

"Good," said the zebra. "If there's one thing we can't stand, it's a carnivore."

"And we've got plenty of them in Short seat," said another, "as I expect you know."

"Flipping lions!" said a third.

"I thought I heard one just as I arrived yesterday," said Hezekiah.

"There are dozens of the horrible things," said the first zebra.

"Safely fenced in, I trust?"

"Oh yes," said an ostrich. "We can't see them but we can hear them."

"And smell 'em," said the first zebra.

One of the two giraffes curved its very long neck down as though to smell the camel, but it said nothing.

It seemed to Hezekiah to be waiting for him to

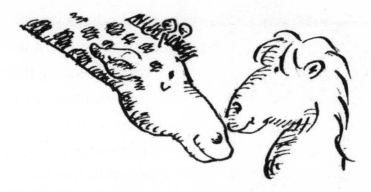

speak, so he asked it, "Do you like living here?"
There was no reply.

"You won't get a word out of him, mate," the
zebras said.

"Why not?"

"They can't talk, giraffes can't."

"A female can make a sort of noise to call her
calf," an ostrich said, "but they can't speak like
we can. Anyway, the answer to your question is
– yes, we all like living here. We've got plenty of
freedom and friends and food."

"And no foes," chorused the zebras.

In the distance, a lion roared.

"Like him," boomed the ostrich.

The sound of the lion seemed to excite all the animals. The zebras heehawed rudely in reply and set off at a gallop, the ostriches sped away at great speed on their powerful legs that ended in huge two-toed feet, and the two giraffes cantered off gracefully together, in perfect step, like dancers.

Left to himself, Hezekiah walked over to a water-trough that stood by the fence and drank a couple of dozen litres of water. Then he heard the noise of motors and looked up to see a Land Rover coming up the road towards him. It was followed by a van marked in large letters BBC FILM UNIT (which meant nothing to Hezekiah), and after that came a pick-up truck loaded with hay (which meant a lot).

When they drew up by him, there stepped from the Land Rover a bearded figure dressed in riding breeches above bright yellow stockings and suede boots and wearing a cowboy hat.

"Good morning, my friend!" said the camel loudly.

"Feed him!" cried the Marquess to the rangers in the pick-up truck. To the film crew who emerged from the van he said, "Here he is, chaps! Isn't he magnificent? Did you ever see anything so hairy?"

The director, the cameraman and the sound recordist all looked at the camel.

Then they looked at the Marquess.

Then they looked at one another.

Then they replied, "No. Never."

CHAPTER EIGHT

As darkness fell, the rangers came to take the camel back to his shed.

"Hezekiah!" they called, and at the sound of his name, he came immediately to them like a well-trained dog, while the zebras, the ostriches and the giraffes watched.

"Blimey! He's obedient!" said the zebras.

"Knows his name," said the ostriches.

The giraffes of course said nothing.

Hezekiah talked to the rangers as they went down the road. "Pretty tiring day I've had," he said. "Those people kept making me stand here and go there while they pointed things at me and at my friend in his funny clothes. I'll be glad to get to bed."

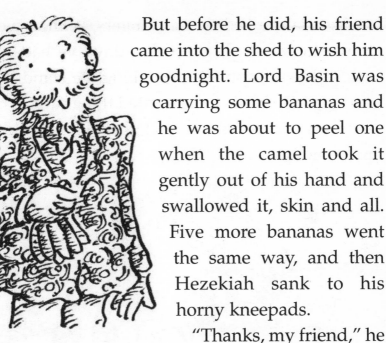

But before he did, his friend came into the shed to wish him goodnight. Lord Basin was carrying some bananas and he was about to peel one when the camel took it gently out of his hand and swallowed it, skin and all. Five more bananas went the same way, and then Hezekiah sank to his horny kneepads.

"Thanks, my friend," he said, "and now if you'll excuse me, I'll get some sleep. I've had a busy day."

In answer to all his rumbles, Lord Basin said, "Get some sleep, old fellow, you've had a busy day."

A pretty successful day too, said the Marquess

to himself as he went back into the great house of Shortseat. Hezekiah got on well with the other beasts, and I should think the BBC people are pleased with their footage.

As he lay in bed that night, clad in purple silk pyjamas, his red nightcap on his head, he suddenly thought that he should have had a go at riding the camel. That would have looked good on film! he said to himself. But would Hezekiah let me sit on him? he thought.

I'm a lot bigger now than when I last had a ride on a camel. Ah well, there's only one way to find out.

Thus it was that next morning when the rangers came to the shed, they did not lead Hezekiah out along the road to his enclosure. Instead they took him into a stable-yard, at one side of which was a stone mounting-block. Standing on this while a horse was led up and stood beside it, it was easy for a rider to step off the block and straddle his steed.

Today the steed was not going to be a horse but (hopefully) a camel. As Hezekiah was led up to the mounting-block, he saw that, standing on it, was his friend, wearing riding breeches and those yellow stockings and various other bright pieces of clothing.

"Now, Hezekiah old chap," his friend said, "I wonder if you will do me a favour?"

He put out a hand to the camel, who gave it that rubbery kiss.

"I shall be so much obliged," said Lord Basin (for politeness costs nothing), "if you'll let me sit on you."

"Tell you what, my friend," said Hezekiah in reply. "Why don't you sit on me and I'll give you a ride?"

What with the kiss and the amiable noises that his camel was making, the Marquess felt confident enough to throw a yellow-stockinged leg over the beast's back.

Hezekiah stood as still as a rock.

Then Lord Basin hoisted himself up off the

mounting-block and sat himself on the broad
hairy back, in between the two hairy humps.

Hezekiah did not move.

Lord Basin looked down at his rangers and
grinned all over his hairy face.

"How about that, eh?" he said to them.
"Splendid, my Lord," they said. "Shall we lead
him on?"

"No, don't bother with the ropes. Just walk on
either side of me and then you can open the gate

291

when we arrive." To Hezekiah he said, "Walk on!"

Being far the tallest, it was the giraffes who first saw the strange procession coming up the road. They could not tell the others, of course, but they cantered over to the fence in such an excited way that the zebras came galloping and the ostriches strode after them.

"Well I never!" said a zebra.

"Did you ever!" said an ostrich.

"Open the gate!" said the Marquess to his rangers.

"Good morning, everyone," said Hezekiah. "I'm giving my friend a ride. He seems to be enjoying it," and he ambled out into the pasture.

The Marquess of Basin sat swaying happily on the camel's back. "Out of the way, you lot!" he shouted to the zebras and ostriches and giraffes, and to Hezekiah, "Trot on!" He took off his cowboy hat and with it gently biffed the camel's flanks. "Giddy-up!" he shouted and Hezekiah broke into a clumsy trot and then the trot became a kind of canter and the canter a sort of gallop.

"Yippee!" yelled Lord Basin as he disappeared into the distance on the back of his big brown bouncing Bactrian camel.

"Well I never!" said one ranger.

"Did you ever!" said the other.

CHAPTER NINE

Later, when Lord Basin had had a shower and changed his clothes, he sat down to his favourite breakfast, a boiled egg. That may not sound much, but it was an *ostrich* egg.

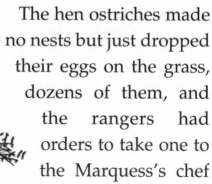

The hen ostriches made no nests but just dropped their eggs on the grass, dozens of them, and the rangers had orders to take one to the Marquess's chef every now and again. The chef would boil the egg for a long time and then, using a small saucepan as an eggcup, set it before Lord Basin, who would eat it with great enjoyment and a tablespoon.

His breakfast finished, the Marquess went to his office. "John," he said to his manager, "I've been thinking."

"Oh yes, sir?"

"About my camel Hezekiah. I've just had a ride on him."

"Really, sir?"

"Yes," said the Marquess. He rubbed his sore bottom absently. Next time, he thought, let's just walk. "I've suddenly realized," he said, "that though he's settled in well at Shortseat and he's healthy and seems quite happy, there is one thing that's missing in his life, and that's a mate. A female Bactrian camel is going to be very hard to find but I want to try, John. I want you to contact every zoo in this country, every zoo in Europe, every zoo in the world indeed, and find out if any of them have a suitable mate for my Hezekiah, and if so, how much they want for her."

"Very well, sir," replied the manager.

Visitors to Shortseat that day found the Marquess of Basin a trifle abstracted. To be sure, he moved among them as usual, courteously answering any questions that they put to him (for politeness costs nothing), dressed in claret-

coloured corduroy trousers, a mauve shirt with a saffron cravat, and a sequinned suede jacket. But they did notice that at intervals he rubbed his bottom and the more observant among them felt that the nobleman had something on his mind. He did. As soon as he could, he returned to his office.

"Any luck, John?" he asked his manager.

"Afraid not, sir."

"No one's got a Bactrian camel?"

"Haven't found one yet."

"Keep trying. Though if we do find a female and if they're willing to sell, they'll ask a huge amount of money. Maybe I can barter for her, but I haven't any more white tigers to spare." Then Lord Basin had a brainwave.

There was a lake at Shortseat, and on the lake was an island, and on the island lived a little family of gorillas, a silverback male, his mate, and their son.

"Tell you what, John," said the Marquess. "We need to find a home for our young gorilla."

The phone rang.

"For you, sir," said the manager.

"Hullo?" said the Marquess.

"We are told that you are looking for a female Bactrian camel, and we have one here," said the speaker (and he mentioned the name of a famous American zoo). "It occurred to us that you might be interested in an idea that we've had."

"I might," said the Marquess.

"No doubt you have

the occasional spare creature at Shortseat, and perhaps there's one that might interest us."

"An exchange, d'you mean?"

"Yes, sir."

"All right," said Lord Basin. "How would you like a few lions?"

"No, thanks."

"Oh. Can you hold on a minute?"

"Sure."

The Marquess winked at his manager and held up one hand, fingers crossed.

"I've just had a brainwave," he said to the caller. "How would you like a gorilla?"

"A gorilla!"

"Yes, a young male."

"In exchange for our young female Bactrian camel?"

"Yes. Straight swap. What do you say?" and the answer was:

"Done!"

CHAPTER TEN

For people to cross the Atlantic by air from America to England (or vice versa) takes very little time. But to transport by sea a gorilla going westward or a Bactrian camel going eastward is not something that can be done in a hurry. So it

Dick King-Smith

was springtime before Lord Basin had news of the arrival date of of Hezekiah's proposed mate.

She must have a suitable name, thought the Marquess. I'll consult the vicar.

"Do you happen to know, Vicar," he said to him the following Sunday, "the name of the wife of Hezekiah?"

"D'you mean Hezekiah the King of Judah?" the vicar asked. "Lived about seven hundred BC?"

"That's the one, I expect," said the Marquess.

"As a matter of fact, I do, Lord Basin."

"What was it?"

"Hephzibah."

"Splendid, splendid! I like it!" cried the Marquess. "Could you spell it for me?"

"I'll write it down," said the vicar.

"I've got a camel called Hezekiah, you see, and though he doesn't know it, he's got a mate arriving next week."

"How nice," said the vicar. "Bless them."

"Thanks so much, Vicar," said Lord Basin. "Bye."

*

The spring that year was everything it should be. The young green grass grew apace, the trees burst into leaf, the birds were singing their heads off, the skies were blue, the sun shone.

In the West Country, visitors poured into Shortseat, to see the famous lions, to see all the many other animals, and even to catch sight occasionally of the Marquess of Basin riding on his camel. Hezekiah always kept to a steady walk now, and his rider sat upon a large comfortable cushion wedged between the camel's two humps and doffed his cowboy hat to passing visitors.

Now that the weather was warmer, Hezekiah no longer slept in his old shed but stayed out with his companions. There was a lot of hee-hawing as the zebra stallions courted their mares, and a lot of booming as the male ostrich pranced about and flapped his wings before his two hens. The giraffes of course were silent, but they stayed very close to one another, sometimes entwining their long necks in token of their love.

Elsewhere, all the animals of Shortseat were enjoying the springtime, from the two gorillas, alone now on the lake island, to the herds of antelopes and the pride of lions.

Only Hezekiah had no companion of his own kind.

One morning when he was giving his friend a ride, he spoke to him about it. "I wish I had a mate," he groaned. "Everyone else has, but I'm on my tod."

"What's up, Hezekiah?" said the Marquess. "You sound a bit down in the mouth. But you just wait, old chap, just wait till this afternoon. You're going to get the shock of your life."

That afternoon (you won't be surprised to hear) Hezekiah got the shock of his life. He was resting comfortably on his horny kneepads beside the water trough, from which he'd just drunk a great deal, when he saw a cattle lorry coming up the road, followed by a Land Rover.

From the lorry a ranger got out and opened the gate and then the driver backed the vehicle into the gateway.

From the Land Rover emerged the brightly dressed figure of the Marquess of Basin, and between them, he and the ranger undid the clips that held up the tailboard, and let it down.

Hezekiah got to his feet, curious to know what newcomer was being put into the enclosure.

"What have you got in there?" he said to his friend the Marquess.

"Guess what we've got in here, Hezekiah old chap!" said Lord Basin. "Come on, Hephzibah, out you come!" Before Hezekiah's astonished eyes, down the tailboard there walked with stately steps a beautiful brown hairy young female Bactrian camel.

"Hullo," she said to him. "I'm Hephzibah. Who are you?"

"I'm Hezekiah," said Hezekiah, and they moved towards each

311

other till their rubbery lips met in a kind of kiss.

"Love at first sight!" said the Marquess of Basin to the ranger. "I do like happy endings!"

Don't you?

THE END

Dick King-Smith

Horse Pie

Illustrated by Valerie Littlewood

Chapter One

"She'll have to go," said the donkeyman.

"Who?" said his son, Sam.

"Old Jenny. She's got so slow. Didn't you see that kid just now trying to make her walk a bit faster?

She was miles behind the others. She's past it."

Sam squiggled sand between his bare toes as he looked at the line of donkeys, waiting patiently for their next riders.

"What will happen to her, Dad?" he said.

"Have to see if they've got room for her at the Donkey Sanctuary," said his father.

"And if they haven't?"

"Cats' meat, I'm afraid," said the donkeyman.

"You mean . . . ?"

"Yes. Have to send the old girl to

the slaughterhouse."

"Oh, Dad, you couldn't! Not old Jenny!" Sam pleaded.

"Well, you think of a better idea then."

"Have a look at this," said the Manager of the Old Horses' Home to his stableman, a couple of days later.

"What is it, boss?"

"Letter from a kid. Son of the chap that keeps the beach donkeys at Easton-super-Mare."

The stableman read the letter.

"'. . . Donkey Sanctuary full up . . .

slaughterhouse . . . you are her last hope . . . Please, please!' Oh dear, pulls at your heart-strings, doesn't it, boss?"

The Manager nodded.

"He can't bear to think of her going to the knackers. We can make room for her, can't we?"

"Sure, boss," said the stableman. "What's one more among so many?"

*

And indeed there were a great many animals in the large, tree-shaded field in front of the Old Horses' Home. They were of all shapes and sizes, and all possible colours, and most of them were well past their prime. But amongst all the ancient ponies and horses were three giants who were, in fact, not old.

Captain and Ladybird were Shire horses, one black, one brown, and both with white stockings. Herbert was a Suffolk Punch – a chestnut like all his kind. All three were in good health but there was no work for them to do – tractors had taken their places.

Far larger and heavier and stronger than the rest, Captain and Ladybird and Herbert looked down their great Roman noses at all the other horses in the place.

One afternoon, the three giants stood side by side under a sycamore tree, watching as a horsebox came up the drive.

"Another old crock, I suppose," said Captain.

"A broken-down nag, I expect," said Ladybird.

"Or a cow-hocked pony," said Herbert.

They moved with ponderous

dignity towards the gate at the top corner of the field. Here the horsebox had stopped, and the stableman, who had come out to meet it, was opening the gate for it to reverse in.

Captain and Ladybird and Herbert watched as the tailgate was lowered. Then they shook their great heads in disgust as down it walked an old grey donkey.

"Good afternoon," she said. "My name is Jenny."

"It is not a good afternoon," said Captain.

"And as far as we are concerned,"

said Herbert, "your name is mud."

"You may not be aware," said Ladybird in the most patronizing of voices, "that this is a Home for horses."

"And not," said Captain, "for whatever sort of animal you may be."

"I think," said Herbert, blowing a snort of disgust through his large nostrils, "that it's an ass."

"Come away, boys," said Ladybird, "and leave the wretched creature. You don't know where it's been."

All three turned and walked

majestically back to the shade of the
sycamore tree.

CHAPTER TWO

Jenny stood watching the three big horses sadly. She thought of all her friends left behind on the beach, and she stretched out her neck and gave a series of creaking, groaning heehaws – the loudest,

most mournful noise imaginable.

Many of the other horses and ponies in the field looked up at this sound, and one animal detached itself from the herd and came over to the donkey. It was a little old skewbald pony, bony and swaybacked, and it walked right up to Jenny and touched noses with her and said in a croaky voice, "Welcome."

"I don't think I am," Jenny said. "Those big horses were horrid to me."

"Don't take no notice," said the skewbald pony. "They'm like that, them three. My name's Alfie, by the way."

"I'm Jenny."

"Toffee-nosed lot they are," said Alfie, nodding his head towards the sycamore tree and the three huge rumps, one black, one brown, one chestnut, of Captain and Ladybird and Herbert. "And they're big-headed with it, not to mention the size of their backsides."

"They are rather fat," said Jenny.

"Fat as butter," said Alfie. "Just the job for the rustlers."

"What are they?"

"Horse-thieves. Chaps that do

come round and nick horses."

"How do you know about these rustlers?" said Jenny.

"Heard tell about them from an old grey mare that used to live here. Dead now she is, but I can remember her telling me about these men that come round, at night usually, and steal livestock – cattle, sheep or horses. Once she saw a whole flock of sheep loaded up into a lorry and driven away."

"But why would they want to steal those three big horses?"

"To ship 'em across the water. To France – it's not far. Be worth their while to come for those three great lumps of lard. Why, they must weigh nearly a tonne apiece," said Alfie.

"But what would they send them to France for?" asked Jenny.

"For meat," said Alfie. "Didn't you know they eat horses in France?"

Jenny let out another ear-shattering bray.

"Eat *horses*!" she said. "How dreadful!"

"Oh, I don't know," Alfie said. "After all, your Englishman eats beef and lamb and pork. It's just that he wouldn't think of eating horses. He'd sooner keep 'em in a Home like this, costing hundreds of pounds to be looked after. But your Frenchman, he's got more sense. He sees a nice fat horse and he thinks to himself, '*Ooh là là!* Horse-pie!'"

"Do the French eat donkeys?" Jenny said.

"I don't reckon so," Alfie said.

"They wouldn't eat you, old girl, nor me, nor any of the old hat-racks round here. We'm all skin and bone. The rustlers wouldn't look at us, so don't worry your head about that."

But Jenny did worry. She was a

kindly animal by nature, and the thought of the possible danger to Captain and Ladybird and Herbert upset her very much. Rude and overbearing they might be, but the idea of those magnificent creatures being stolen and taken away by lorry and then by ship to France, there to be killed and made into horse-pie – that was horrifying!

CHAPTER THREE

For the rest of that day Jenny could think of nothing else as she grazed her way about the big field in Alfie's company.

Alfie, she noticed, though among the smallest of the ponies, was obviously a figure of some importance. He introduced her to the others as they met, and on the whole they greeted her in a friendly fashion. Though when a mare with a bit of breeding about her said, "An ass! What next?" she soon regretted it, for Alfie wheeled, quick as a cat, and his hind hooves beat a tattoo on her ribs.

But the three great carthorses were a different matter. One after another they worked their way close to the donkey and then, suddenly, lashed out or tried to bite her back. Once they lined up together and galloped

across the field towards her, snorting and whinnying, as though they meant to squash her into the very ground.

"Let's hope the rustlers get you!" shouted Alfie as they dodged out of the way. "Horse-pie, that's all you're good for!" But, of course, the thunder of hooves drowned his words.

"These rustlers," Jenny said. "When do they come?"

"At night," said Alfie. "Likely they'll have a big cattle-lorry parked down on the road, and then they'll come up the drive on foot, with halters."

"And how will they catch Captain and Ladybird and Herbert?"

"Sugar-lumps, I shouldn't wonder," said Alfie. "They'll go anywhere for a sugar-lump, they will. All the way to France, in fact."

"Alfie," said Jenny. "We must stop them."

"Stop who?"

"The rustlers."

"Whatever for, old girl? Good riddance to bad rubbish, I says. Nasty-tempered great things."

"I don't care about that," said Jenny. "They're still English horses and I'm an English donkey, and I'm not having them made into French horse-pies. We must stop the rustlers."

"Oh, nothing easier," said Alfie acidly. "You just waits by the gate and when the rustlers open it, you nips out and down the drive, and then you punctures all the tyres on the cattle-lorry."

"How do I do that?"

"Bite 'em."

For answer Jenny rolled back her lips, and Alfie could see that what few teeth she had left were blunt and brown and broken.

"Oh," he said. "Perhaps not."

"No," said Jenny, "but you've given me an idea."

"What?"

"'When the rustlers open the gate,' you said."

"Well?"

"There's only one gate to this field. There's no other way for Captain and Ladybird and Herbert to be taken out. The post-and-rail fence is too high, even if they could be made to jump it.

"So?"

"We wait until the rustlers are in the field with their halters and their sugar-lumps, and then we block the gate."

"You're joking, old girl," said Alfie. "You and me, stood in the gateway, trying to stop the rustlers leading those three monsters through? We'd get killed."

"We might," said Jenny, "but we needn't be alone. All the other horses and ponies could help. The

rustlers couldn't get through the whole herd."

The stableman, coming out to have a look round his horses, saw the skewbald pony and the donkey standing nose to nose. The pony was nodding his head vigorously.

"You've got something there, Jenny," Alfie said. "But they'd drive us out of the way after a bit. We shall need help from the stableman. How're we going to get him up in the middle of the night?"

"That's easy," Jenny said. "You leave that bit to me."

CHAPTER FOUR

"It's a funny thing, boss," said the stableman to the Manager of the Home, some days later, "but those horses are acting ever so strange. Every evening at dusk they gather round the gateway, in a tight mass,

and then after a bit they move away,
but not too far away. It's almost as if
they were practising something."

"All of them?" the Manager said.
"They all do this?"

"Not Captain or Ladybird or Herbert," the stableman said. "They don't seem to be part of it."

"Beneath their dignity perhaps," the Manager said.

"I watched particularly last night," the stableman said, "and it's old Alfie and that donkey that seem to be the ringleaders. They go around from horse to horse, and then the whole lot move over to the gateway. It's since that donkey came."

"Funny," said the Manager, "but you've reminded me of something. There's talk of rustlers in the district."

"Taking horses?"

"Yes. For the French trade. Put a stout chain and padlock on that gate, will you? It's the only one into the field."

That evening, Jenny and Alfie watched as the stableman carried out his orders.

"That's all right then," Jenny said.

"If the rustlers do come, they won't be able to get in."

"Be your age," said Alfie. "No, on second thoughts don't, you're old enough as it is. But they'll cut through that chain in a jiffy. They're professionals, these chaps, they know what to expect. Mark my words."

Alfie's words were marked a week later.

The evening parade of the herd around the gateway had just been dismissed, and only Alfie and Jenny still stood there in the dusk.

Suddenly Alfie put his muzzle against Jenny's long, hair-filled ear. "Look," he said softly.

They watched as a shadowy figure came walking up the drive. The man, they could see as he neared them, looked quite respectable – just an ordinary chap taking an evening stroll.

He stopped at the gate and leaned upon it, and looked about the darkening field. There was just enough light left to show, in their usual place beneath the sycamore, the three giant shapes.

"Watch," said Alfie as the man, after looking carefully around, put out a hand to examine the chain and padlock. Then he turned and went silently back.

"A rustler?" Jenny said.

"Looks like it. Haven't heard no lorry yet, it's too early."

"Shall we tell the others?" said Jenny. "We could always block the gateway to stop them getting in."

"No, no," said Alfie. "We wants them to come in and then we'll stop them getting out. Catch 'em red-handed. You go on down to the bottom by the road, old girl, and listen out for a lorry. Your ears are bigger than mine."

CHAPTER FIVE

Jenny was dozing by the rails when, around midnight, she heard a cattle-lorry approaching. It parked just outside the fence, on the grass verge of the road. Its lights were switched off and three men got out and very

quietly lowered the tailboard.

Jenny made off up the field.

"Look at that old moke!" one of the men said. "She's a walking skeleton."

"Don't think we'll bother with her," said a second man.

"Wait till you see the heavy horses," the third man said. "Why, they must weigh nearly a tonne apiece. Come on now, let's get a move on. I've got the bolt-cutters."

It was a darkish night, and the rustlers did not notice that, by the time they reached the gate, all the horses and ponies were alert, watching. The bolt-cutters made short

357

work of the chain, and the men opened the gate, came into the field, closed the gate again, and set off towards the sycamore tree with their halters and their sugar-lumps. Behind them, the herd closed silently in front of the gateway.

Minutes passed, and then the horses saw the three rustlers making their

way back towards the gate. Behind each man walked a giant haltered shape, mumbling a sugar-lump.

"Right," said Alfie. "Stand firm, everybody." At his words, the ancients closed ranks even more tightly. Some faced the enemy, their yellow old teeth ready to bite. Some turned tail, prepared to kick the living daylights out of the rustlers. All stood waiting, dogged and determined.

"Get out of the way," the rustlers called, as quietly as they could. "Get out of it, you pack of miserable old deadbeats."

No-one moved.

Then Alfie's shrill neigh rang out.

"Captain! Ladybird! Herbert!" he cried. "Run for it! They're taking you to France, to make you into horse-pie!" At his words the three whirled away, dragging the halter-ropes from the men's hands, and

thundered off across the field.

"Now, Jenny!" called Alfie, and from inside the donkey's aged frame came those awful creaking, groaning heehaws, loud enough to wake the dead.

The stableman woke with a start.
"Listen!" he said to his wife. "The
old donkey's braying, in the middle
of the night. That's not natural.

Something's wrong. Dial nine-
nine-nine for the police. I'll get my
gun," and he jumped out of bed.

Out in the field, the rustlers stood
undecided, swearing, but Alfie had

not done with them yet.

"Charge!" he cried, and now the whole herd of horses set off, straight at the rustlers, who threw themselves wildly over the fence and ran madly down the drive, pursued by the stableman. On the road a police car drew up beside the cattle-lorry.

CHAPTER SIX

Down on the beach at Easton-super-Mare, the donkeyman leaned against one of his charges, reading the local newspaper. Suddenly he called to his son.

"Hey, Sam!" he cried. "Look at this!"

DONKEY FOILS RUSTLERS – DRAMA AT OLD HORSES' HOME

A warning from an old donkey led to the arrest of three horse-thieves who were attempting to steal stock from the Old Horses' Home. As luck would have it, the donkey chanced to bray loudly in the middle of the night and thus give the alarm. The police were able to intercept the rustlers, who will appear before local magistrates next week.

"That's got to be our old Jenny, Dad!" said Sam. "It must be. She's the only donkey in the place."

"Wonder how she knew they were rustlers," said the donkeyman. "What a funny thing."

*

"Funny thing," said the Manager of the Old Horses' Home to the stableman as they stood by the gate, a couple of days later. "The two Shires and the Suffolk Punch seem to have taken quite a fancy to that old donkey. They never went near her before except to rough her up."

"I know," said the stableman. "Look at them all now, boss, standing together under the sycamore tree, chummy as can be. It's almost as though they realized that they owe their lives to her. But of course they couldn't possibly know that."

Just then they heard a snickering beside them, and turned to see the old skewbald pony, baring his yellow teeth in what looked like a grin.

"Hello, Alfie," said the stableman. "What are you laughing at?"

THE END

❖ ABOUT THE AUTHOR ❖

DICK KING-SMITH was a Gloucestershire farmer until the age of 45, when he gave up farming to become a primary school teacher. His first book, *The Fox Busters*, was published in 1978, and he went on to become a prolific and bestselling full-time author, writing well over a hundred books. His work received many awards, including a Smarties Prize Bronze Medal for *All Because of Jackson* and the Children's Book Award for *Harriet's Hare*, and he was also voted Children's Author of the Year in 1992. His top-selling title *The Sheep-Pig* was developed into the Academy Award nominated movie *Babe*. He passed away in 2011 at the age of 88.

❧ FUNNY FRANK ❧

"I've got a chicken that wants to be a duck!"

Frank is a funny chick. Unlike all his brothers and sisters, he doesn't want to peck around at anything and everything in the dust. No, Frank wants to dabble about in the lovely duck pond, splashing himself with water. Most of all, he wants to learn to swim.

Can Jemima, the farmer's daughter, find a way to help Frank? And if Frank can swim like a duck, what will happen when he grows up to be a cockerel?

978 0 552 55436 7

❧ HAPPY MOUSEDAY ❧

"You are NOT keeping a mouse in this house!"

Every Saturday - or Mouseday, as Pete calls it –
Pete asks his mum and dad if he can have a pet mouse.
And every week, the answer is the same. No.
Then Pete gets a terrific idea. He could secretly
keep a mouse in his tree-house . . .

978 0 552 52820 7

❧ THE ADVENTUROUS SNAIL ❧

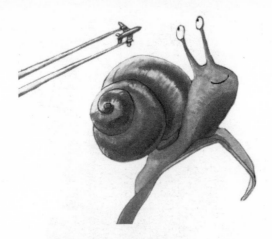

Snail on board!

Siegfried loves to explore. One day his explorations
take him on a big adventure – from his home in the
grass, to the airport, on to an aeroplane and
all the way to America!

There he makes some very important friends,
Mr Ambassador and Mr President, finds a new
home in a sandwich box – and also meets
the lovely Peggy Sue . . .

978 0 552 55045 1

🐾 TITUS RULES OK 🐾

"Titus, my boy," said the Queen, "I have a funny feeling
that you are going to be a very special dog."

Titus is a young corgi puppy, growing up in Windsor
Castle. There is lots he must learn (like how not to
trip up Prince Philip!). Soon he becomes the Queen's
favourite, and she even lets him sleep on her bed
at night! And it is because of Titus that Her Majesty
finally does something very surprising . . .

978 0 552 55431 2